THE MARRIAGE CEREMONY

To Clorinda, it was like a dream—no, a nightmare; and she went through it with a sense of unreality.

To the Duke, it was boring. He was perfectly dressed, unlike his dowdy bride. He had chosen to array himself in knee breeches. His high collar and snowy white stock were arranged in intricate folds. The only touch of jewelry about him was a heavy gold seal upon the fourth finger of his left hand.

Clorinda had to crook her third finger so the gold wedding band which was too large would not fall off. Was it a bad omen? All she knew as she walked down the aisle with this man who was a total stranger was that it was not the wedding she had dreamed of. She was not meant to be wed in an old dress of her mother's, hastily altered to her size, nor was she meant to be the bride. She was the younger Villiers daughter, not the elder whom the Duke had asked to marry. She had red hair, not the dismal yellow it had turned when she had tried to bleach it. What was apparent to her was that although she was not the bride he had arranged for, the Duke didn't even care . . .

Novels by Caroline Courtney

Duchess in Disguise
A Wager For Love

Published by
WARNER BOOKS

CAROLINE COURTNEY

DUCHESS IN DISGUISE

WARNER BOOKS

A Warner Communications Company

WARNER BOOKS EDITION

Copyright © 1979 by Caroline Courtney
All rights reserved.

ISBN 0-446-94050-X

This Warner Books Edition is published by
arrangement with Arlington Books (Publishers) Ltd.

Cover design by Gene Light

Cover art by Walter Popp

Warner Books, Inc., 75 Rockefeller Plaza, New York, N.Y. 10019

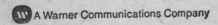 A Warner Communications Company

Printed in the United States of America

Not associated with Warner Press, Inc. of Anderson, Indiana

First Printing: June, 1979

10 9 8 7 6 5 4 3 2 1

(1)

The two curly heads bent over the letter were radiantly fair—one the pale yellow of primrose, the other the burnished red-gold of flame. Both girls were dressed very simply in white muslin gowns cut high at the neck, without any frills or furbelows.

They were sitting arm in arm upon the window seat of a room that had obviously seen better days. The shafts of sunlight that poured in through the window picked out faded hangings and signs of wear on the furniture. A touch of black gave a sombre note to the otherwise idyllic scene. Both girls were wearing a black ribbon for mourning in their locks.

"What shall we do?" sighed the elder Miss de Villiers. A perfect blonde with azure blue eyes and a profile worthy of a Grecian coin, Emily de Villiers was the acknowledged beauty of the neighborhood for miles around. "Incomparable" was what her admirers called her.

Yet though Emily was so beautiful, she was not at all conceited. Indeed she was of a gentle and timid nature. Somehow she always seemed to turn to her younger sister for advice. "I wish Mama was still alive," she continued. "What can we do about this letter?"

"We shall reply, of course," was the firm answer which came from the girl beside her. Clorinda de Villiers was not yet out in society and had none of her elder sister's classic good looks. Yet there was a fiery charm about her. Her flame-gold locks were too long for fashion, and fell nearly to her waist in untidy tendrils. Her nose was too uptilted for perfection, and three small freckles upon its end gave her face an elfin quality. No amount of cucumber water or crushed fresh strawberries could get rid of those freckles.

But it was her eyes that gave character to her face. They were green, glowing pools of mystery, so large that they dominated all her other features.

"We shall reply, of course," she repeated. "The Duke obviously knows nothing of Mama's death, so we shall just sign her name to the letter. It will be simpler than explaining."

"Would that be right?" asked Emily.

"It would be quite all right." Clorinda's eyes flashed with indignation. "The Duke has not even bothered to ask after Mama's health. He clearly does not know or care. Anyway, what else can we do? We cannot get one of the servants to write."

As she spoke, she felt unbidden tears well into her eyes. Her gentle, uncomplaining mother had been an invalid ever since her husband, Sir Harry de Villiers, had died three years earlier. The de Villiers family was an ancient one, able to trace the baronetcy back for hundreds of years. Their pedigree stretched even farther, right back to the Saxon kings, years before the Normans had even thought of invading Britain.

Yet there had never been the money to go with the pedigree. Those three years on a widow's jointure had taxed Lady de Villier's gay spirit to its utmost. Only the week before, she had followed the husband she adored to his last resting place, in the family tomb at the small churchyard of Villiers-sub-Arden.

"Do we dare do that?" Emily's question interrupted Clorinda's wistful reverie.

"Do you dare do what?" asked a man's voice, as their elder brother, Jack, walked into the room. Like Emily, he was fair-haired and good-looking. But, unlike his sisters, he bore the marks of dissipation on his face. Sir John de Villiers, known to his cronies as Jack, had come into the title before he was twenty and had acquired with it a tendency to riotous living.

He was carelessly dressed in the buckskin breeches and riding boots that were the mark of a gentleman in the country. Flinging his lanky limbs over one of the old drawing room chairs, he demanded, "What romps are you plotting now, Clorinda?" For a moment a smile flickered across his face, and he looked younger than his twenty-two years.

"We are not plotting anything, Jack," replied his youngest sister furiously. "Anyway none of my romps, as you call them, can compare with your gambling debts. We were just discussing what to do about this letter which came for Mama. It's a proposal of marriage for Emily from some Duke who has never even met her. He obviously hasn't read about Mama's death in *The Gazette* either. So I think we just ought to reply as if it comes from Mama."

"Give me the letter. I am head of the family now, Clorinda—not you." Jack seized the piece of paper and rapidly scanned it. Then he gave a low whis-

7

tle. He got up from the chair and went over and kissed Emily with brotherly awkwardness.

"Congratulations, Emily," he said. "You will be very rich. It's the Duke of Westhampton, and a splendid match. He is as rich as Croesus, and one of the greatest dandies in the fashionable world."

Emily blushed but she said nothing.

It was left to seventeen-year-old Clorinda to reply. "Goodness, Jack. Emily wouldn't like that at all," she said in her forthright way. "Have you forgotten that she is going to marry Robert Willoughby? If it wasn't for Mama's illness, the engagement would have been announced by now."

"I haven't forgotten," came the reply. "You are only a child, Clorinda. The Duke of Westhampton's offer is more than this family deserves. Willoughby is just a younger son of a country squire. How can his offer compare?"

"But he and Emily are in love," objected Clorinda.

"Emily knows what her duty to the family must be, even if you don't," retorted Jack. "You are being naive, Clorinda. We are practically penniless, and only a good marriage can save me from a debtor's prison, and you from having to earn your living as a governess. I was at my wits' end what to do until I saw this letter."

"It's true, dearest Clorinda," said Emily softly. "For a moment I forgot everything but my love for Robert. But I can't refuse this offer. It is my duty to you both. The Duke will pay off all our debts if I marry him, and besides, then I can give you a proper coming out ball in London. I shall have to tell Robert . . ." Her voice broke off, suspended in tears.

"I think it is mercenary and disgusting," said

Clorinda vigorously. "Why should you be sacrificed for me and Jack, just because Jack keeps betting on all the wrong horses? I would rather like being a governess anyway. I don't want you to be miserable."

"At least Emily will be miserable in the lap of luxury," said her brother dryly. "You are unfair, Clorinda. It is not just my debts that have ruined us. There were Papa's too, and Mama knew nothing about money. I am afraid some of her debts will come to light too. One of us will simply have to marry a fortune within the next few weeks, otherwise we shall have the bailiffs at Villiers Manor, itself."

There was silence for a moment. A large tear rolled down Emily's cheek. Jack was right, thought Clorinda. Her angelic Mama had been a baby where money was concerned. Even though she was the youngest in the family, it had been Clorinda who had tried to teach her mother that money should not be spent so recklessly. She had scrimped and saved, trying to reduce their expenses, only to discover that her mother had ordered coral necklaces for her two daughters. Clorinda sighed with the memory.

"I suppose it is true that one of us must marry money," she said thoughtfully. "It can't be you, Jack, because Lizzie Appleby is the only heiress we know, and she wouldn't have you. She's never forgotten the time you put a frog down her neck when you were eight. But why does it have to be Emily? Give me that letter to read again."

Smoothing out the by now crumpled paper, she read it aloud.

The Duke of Westhampton presents his compliments. He is desirous of allying his Family with the de Villiers, and understands that you have a suitable daughter of Marriageable Age. He therefore requests the hand of Miss de Villiers in the hope that the Marriage may be celebrated with all possible Speed.

Looking round triumphantly at her brother, Clorinda concluded, "It doesn't say which daughter and it doesn't mention Emily by name. So why shouldn't I marry him instead of Emily? Then she can be happy with Robert, and Jack's debts will be paid and the family's fortunes retrieved." Her enormous eyes sparkled with satisfaction at the thought of this solution.

"You," said Jack with scorn. "You're not even 'out.' Besides you don't even look like a de Villiers with all that red hair. And you're only seventeen. The Duke won't want a nursery Miss as a bride."

"I can change the color of my hair," said Clorinda. "I shall bleach it or something. Since we've always lived in the country neither the Duke nor anybody else will know what to expect. And if I dress up in some of Mama's dresses I shall look much older."

"Oh, Clorinda," Emily's voice was suffused with tears. "If only you could . . . but I'm afraid he would find out."

"Why should he? I shall write back, as if from Mama, saying that due to my illness I cannot come up to London. I shall say that my daughter Clorinda will marry him, as long as he is willing to have a quiet wedding, and that I shall send her up to London for it. Why should the Duke care? He hasn't even bothered to find out what your name is, Emily. Isn't that proof that he just wants a marriage of convenience, with no question of love?"

"I don't like it," Jack frowned. "Oh, I'll admit the scheme might work, but what about you, Clorinda? What will you feel like getting married? And what will you tell the Duke afterwards?"

"I shall tell him the truth, of course." Clorinda stood up proudly. "One of us has got to marry him, you said so yourself Jack. I am not in love like Emily is. I am the practical member of the family. Mama always said so. She used to call Emily her 'fairy daughter' and me her 'household elf daughter'."

With a determined toss of her flaming hair, she faced them both. In her simple muslin dress, and the black ribbon in her hair, she looked absurdly young. The thin material fell in soft folds over a body that had not yet achieved the voluptuous curves of womanhood. Her slender shoulders were braced, though, like those of a soldier. But for the glittering green pools of her eyes, she might have been a young boy setting out on life for the first time.

Perhaps it was the vulnerable look of his sister that made even careless Jack uneasy. "You're too young," he said. "What do you know about marriages of convenience and how to behave in high society?"

"I know what it means," said his sister proudly. "A marriage of convenience is one in which the husband continues to have his opera dancers and his wife pretends she does not know about them. Mama always said that gentlemen were different in that way."

"Oh, Clorinda, surely you didn't ask her about things like that," said Emily, shocked at the very thought. "I am sure she cannot have said anything of the kind. She never even mentioned such things when I said I was marrying Robert."

"Robert is different and so are you, my darling sister." Clorinda tightened her arm about her sister's waist. "You two are *in love.*"

"But what about you, Clorinda?" said Emily trying to be fair. "You might fall in love."

"Not me," said the girl firmly. "I'm never going to do anything of the kind."

"Please, Jack," whispered Emily, convinced. "Let Clorinda write the letter. If the Duke agrees to the match without seeing us, it will mean he cannot care which sister he weds. If not, I promise to do my duty for the sake of the family."

Jack still looked uneasy. He began walking up and down the sun-lit room in perplexity. Then his rather dissolute face broke into a boyish grin. "I agree, Clorinda. You can write the letter. I must say I should give odds to see the Duke's face when he discovers he has the younger, not the elder sister. I wager it will be the first time he has ever been outwitted by a woman."

"I am sure the Duke of Westhampton is very lucky to be marrying Clorinda," said Emily loyally. "Besides he will be allying himself to one of the oldest families in Britain. The Villiers are much older than the Westhamptons, you know."

"A good pedigree's never done me much good," said Jack. "Ah well, Clorinda, I'll say this. You have turned up veritable trumps, dear sister. I'll be back to London in the meantime. Winterstoke tells me there's a new gaming club been opened."

"I do wish you would stop playing with that awful Lord Winterstoke," said Emily. "You seem always to lose money when you are with him."

"Winterstoke's the most knowing man in London," said her brother shortly. He turned to leave the room.

The two sisters looked at each other in despair. Jack's passion for gambling had been a worry in the family for the last three years. "And the trouble is," said Clorinda when he had gone, "he has the devil's own bad luck."

"You shouldn't use such phrases, darling," said Emily in rebuke. "They are not ladylike. But I'm afraid I know what you mean. I fear that dear Papa was much the same."

The next few days brought bad news for the two girls. Their mother's business affairs, it seemed, were in a worse state than even Jack had foreseen. Lady de Villiers had invested her small funds in speculative stocks, and there was only enough left to pay off the family servants the wages they were owed, and to settle a few trifling debts around the neighborhood.

Lady de Villiers had never been prudent about money. Indeed she had despised it. "Never marry for money," she had told the girls. "Only love can make you happy."

Whenever Clorinda thought of those words, a cold shiver went down her spine. Had she made a horrible mistake by offering to marry the Duke? Then she would think of Jack's debts and gentle Emily's love for Robert, and she would think again. "I may be a girl," she said to herself, "but I can face difficulties and overcome them as well as any boy."

While she waited for the Duke's answer, Clorinda spent much of her time in the quiet Villiers Manor library. Sometimes she could hardly help crying when she looked round all the familiar leatherbound volumes, battered from so much use. She knew and loved them all. Jack had been sent to Eton, of course, but the two girls had been left to pick up their education as they liked. Unlike some families they had never employed a governess. There never seemed the funds.

Instead, Clorinda had spent many hours in the library browsing among the books, and, with the help of the local parson, trying to keep up with Jack's studies in Latin and Greek. Emily had never been bookish, but Clorinda was just the opposite. She could lose herself and her daily worries in the writings of the great authors like Shakespeare.

It was a Saturday when she was browsing among the books, that she suddenly remembered her mother taking a book from the shelves and saying to her, "Clorinda, let me read you this passage from Shakespeare. I know you will enjoy it. It is one of the finest passages of poetry in the English language."

Irresistably she was drawn to the same shelf, and to the very same volume. As if to remind her, it fell open at the same passage.

> *To be or not to be: that is the question:*
> *Whether 'tis nobler in the mind to suffer*
> *The slings and arrows of outrageous fortune,*
> *Or to take arms against a sea of troubles*
> *And by opposing end them?"*

"Perhaps that is what I am doing?" thought Clorinda, "taking arms against a sea of troubles instead of just letting them overwhelm the family." Somehow the thought comforted her.

She was interrupted by Emily, who came in at a run. "Oh Clorinda, it's come," she burst out. "The letter, I mean. I dare not open it, so I have brought it to you."

Slowly Clorinda took it from her sister's outstretched and trembling fingers. She discovered that her own hands were not quite steady. What would the letter contain? Would it mean ruin for the family with a refusal? Or the sacrifice of poor Emily's loving heart? Or would it be a demand for her own hand in marriage—a demand which would bring her riches, luxury and a world without love?

She examined the writing. It was different this time, more careless and less tidy than the script on the original letter. "Perhaps his secretary wrote the earlier letter?" she wondered, and felt slightly sick with anger. Or was it fear? She tore the paper open.

For a moment the black scrawl swam before her eyes.

I am obliged for your early Communication," she read. *"Thank you for the offer of your daughter, Clorinda's hand in Marriage. In the circumstances of your illness, a quiet Wedding is no doubt best. It will perfectly meet my own wishes on the Matter. I will await the future Duchess at St. Margaret's, Westminster, on May 10th.* The signature was large and bold—WESTHAMPTON.

"But that's only a week," gasped Emily.

"So much the better," said Clorinda. "It is clear that this is a transaction for him, not an affair of the heart. Why even a Duke, one would think, must inspect a horse before he buys it. Yet the Duke does not think fit to cast an eye over his bride. Well, he will get the Villiers connection. It is clear he cares for nothing else."

15

She was unreasonably angry, she knew. After all, this letter was just what both sisters wanted. Had the Duke insisted on meeting his bride beforehand, then the whole scheme might have been undone.

What had she expected, after all? A love letter? To a girl he had never met and obviously could not care for? She shook herself.

"But, Clorinda," quavered Emily, "what shall we do about your trousseau? May the tenth is only a week away. There will not be time to have Mama's dresses properly altered by a dressmaker."

"We shall just have to do our best, ourselves," said Clorinda. "Besides we have no money to pay a dressmaker."

"But you know that you and I cannot sew well. Oh Clorinda, you will look a perfect fright. And the Duke will be expecting a beauty, no doubt."

"We can't worry about that. We shall just have to do the best we can," said Clorinda firmly. "If you and I set to work, we shall manage a trousseau somehow. Besides, once I am married I shall be able to have all the clothes I want.

"Think of it, Emily," she went on. "I shall be able to buy silk stockings and fans and ribbons and everything. Are you sure you don't want to marry the Duke?"

"Oh no," said Emily shuddering.

"There is one thing I am rather worried about," said Clorinda. "And that is bleaching my hair. I suppose the housemaid can lend me some of the stuff she does her hair with."

"Her hair doesn't look very nice," said Emily in dismay. "It seems rather a pity to spoil your red colored hair."

"It's probably best that I do," said Clorinda. "The

Duke will expect me to be fair like Jack. There's one consolation. I don't care what the Duke thinks. He's bound to turn out to be utterly boring and pompous. I quite hate him already."

* * *

The next few days passed in such a bustle of preparation, that Clorinda barely had time to think at all. With the help of Emily, she turned out their mother's old wardrobe—the first time since her death that the sisters had been through her things.

As they sat in their mother's bedroom, surrounded by all her old dresses and the little treasures of ribbons and lace that she had hoarded, the two sisters could not help but weep. "Do you remember when she had this day dress made?" said Emily, holding up the folds of a pink sarsenet dress.

"I do remember," sighed Clorinda. "Mama looked so beautiful. Do you think we could alter it for my trousseau?" She draped the soft material around herself. The dress had looked exquisite upon her fair-haired mother. The soft pink color had brought out the gentle blue of her eyes. It would look good on Emily too. But on Clorinda the effect of the pink was very different. Somehow it made her burning red-gold hair look tawdry, and the deep green of her eyes faded against the color.

"It doesn't suit you like it suited Mama," said Emily. "Why don't you try this pale mauve gown?"

Clorinda gathered up the dress and held its heavy folds of satin against her. Emily frowned. It still did not look right. The pale mauve clashed with her sister's hair, and made her green eyes look a sort of faded blue.

17

"The mauve isn't any better, darling," she said. "Isn't there anything else?"

Rummaging through the wardrobe, Clorinda pulled out another pink dress, a third of the same color, another mauve dress—and then a gray dress. "Try that one," advised Emily.

"It's rather dull, isn't it?" said Clorinda in a small voice. She was dismayed at the reality of what they were doing. When she had said proudly that her mother's dresses would do for the trousseau, she had not really thought what it would mean. Now with the slight fragrance of her mother's rose water still clinging to the soft fabrics, she could hardly bear it. It seemed almost like sacrilege to dress up in her mother's clothes.

"Wouldn't my best muslin do, the one we keep for Sundays?" she pleaded. "I don't want to have to wear Mama's things."

"Dear Clorinda, I know what you must be going through," said Emily sympathetically. "But I don't think any of your clothes will do. Most of them are my old ones, and very faded."

She spoke the truth. In the last few years, Clorinda had insisted that any money spent on clothes should go on her older beautiful sister, who was "out" in society, rather than on herself, still a girl in the nursery.

"Just try the gray," coaxed Emily.

Reluctantly Clorinda took off her old white muslin, and stepped into the heavy gray silk. It was far too big for her, and underneath its heavy folds her shoulders looked frailer than ever. Yet it was definitely an improvement upon the pinks and mauves, as far as color went. It looked drab, quiet, dull—but at least it didn't clash or look in bad taste.

"I think this one will do, Emily," she said. "At least I can wear it for the wedding. It looks rather old-fashioned, but it makes me look older, I think."

In an odd way, it did. Though her body through the material was pitifully slender, the dress disguised some of its immaturity. Under the heavy material, Clorinda looked frail, but not so young. Nobody could say that the dress suited her, but at least she looked respectable.

"I shall have to wear the pink to travel in," she mused aloud. "But I daresay it will look less frightful when I have bleached my hair."

Bleaching her hair turned out to be more of a problem than the two girls had foreseen. They had borrowed some lotion from one of the housemaids and asked her instructions on how to use it.

Emily washed Clorinda's long locks with the usual herbal mixtures they favored—soapwort and camomile—and then she rubbed in the lotion the housemaid had provided and left it for several minutes. Then she rinsed the hair, and both girls waited anxiously for it to dry in front of the nursery fire.

"It certainly looks lighter already," said Emily.

Clorinda twisted her heavy locks round and stared at them. "It's lighter all right," she admitted. "But it doesn't look very healthy, does it? All the ends are slip and the curl seems to have gone out of it somehow."

Her worst fears were realized when her hair was finally dried. The bleach had worked only too well. What had been lively red-gold, was now a dull yellow and lacking in vitality. Not only the hair, itself, lacking in life, but it seemed to drain the life from Clorinda's complexion and eyes.

"I shall just have to cover my hair whenever possible," said Clorinda aloud. "At least nobody can recognise me."

She was glad she had left the task of bleaching her hair till the last day of her time at Villiers Manor. She had dreaded the moment when she must say goodbye to the house where she had been born. In her eyes there could never be anything more lovely than the red Elizabethan brick and Tudor half timbers of her home. At least bleaching her hair had given herself something other than her departure to worry about.

When the time of parting finally came, she could not hold back her tears. Loyal to the last, Emily had accompanied her to the roadside where the stage coach would pick her up for the journey to London. Jack had sent some money from London—"thanks to the Duke" is how he had put it in his letter. "It won't pay for a private carriage, but I don't like to borrow too much before the wedding bells. I am afraid you will have to take the stage, Clorinda. Mind you behave yourself."

"I wish Jack had escorted you," fussed Emily, as they waited in the slight chill of the morning. "I am not happy about you staying by yourself in an inn, Clorinda."

"Don't worry, Emily," Clorinda reassured her sister. "I am staying in a very respectable place, where they used to know our father. I am better off on my own anyway. You know what Jack is like. Ten to one he would be laying bets on every carriage that passed, or inviting the coachman to join him at cards at every stop in the road."

She added wistfully. "Besides I do not look beautiful enough to attract attention. Who could look twice at me?"

Her words were only too accurate. Over the unbecoming pink day dress, she was wearing a drab beige pelisse whose folds were too ample for her slender form. Her half boots under this were shabby with too much use, and her gloves slightly too large for her. The fur trimmings of the fashionable world, and the huge furry muffs had been beyond the girls' ingenuity. A discreet but aging bonnet completed her ensemble.

Any comforting words her sister might have offered, were halted as the stage coach in a flurry of dust and galloping hooves rounded the corner. Spotting the two figures outside the Manor, the four horses slowed down to a trot, finally halting a little way further on. The guard climbed down and helped Clorinda with her modest leather box, placing it in the basket that hung at the back of the vehicle.

"Climb in, my dear," he said with a friendly smile, for he was a fatherly man.

For a second the two girls clung together in a speechless embrace, then Clorinda tore herself away. From inside the crowded coach, she could just see her sister's solitary figure, till the dust rising from the horses' hooves hid her and Villiers Manor from sight.

It was just before the town where the coach was due to stop for the night, that Clorinda had a lesson in how the truly rich travel. The stage coach had seemed to her untutored eye to be going at a breakneck speed. But as it was rounding a fairly steep bend in the road, to her amazement she realized it was being overtaken. Through the window she perceived the wide-nostriled heads of a perfectly matched pair of gray horses.

They sped by the coach with only an inch to spare at a reckless pace. Clorinda caught her breath in astonishment. Surely only a madman would drive so fast. She craned her neck to see who was the driver and caught a glimpse of a tall dark man wearing a driving coat of many capes. His whole attention was focused on the dangerous maneuver of guiding his curricle past the coach. Then the whole coach swayed dangerously, and the equipage was gone. Only a cloud of dust rising against the window was evidence of the astounding haste of his passing.

A few miles onward, the coach came to a halt at the inn where its passengers were to spend the night. Stiff from her journey, Clorinda climbed out and looked round for a sight of those unforgettable gray horses. She could not see them, nor the dark man who had been driving them. Perhaps he had continued his journey onwards. "What a pity," thought Clorinda. "I should have liked to see those wonderful horses, just so that I could tell Jack about them."

The Queen's Arms, where the coach had halted, was a well-conducted establishment with a courtyard bustling with grooms and ostlers who led away the tired coach horses. Inside was all bustle too, and for a moment Clorinda felt a pang of embarrassment. Then a red-faced innkeeper came up and asked her if she was Miss de Villiers. "I have a bedchamber for you," said he, in tones which made it clear he recognized her as a gentlewoman despite her shabby appearance. "But I am not able to give you a private parlor. Mine has been bespoke by a gentleman who arrived here before the coach," he apologized.

Thinking of her pitifully small store of coins, Clorinda reflected that perhaps this was to her advantage. She thanked the innkeeper politely, and when the harassed landlord was approached by one of the other stage passengers, looked around for somebody to carry her chest. "I will show you your bedchamber, Miss," said a smiling chambermaid and led Clorinda to the small bedchamber that had been reserved for her. There was the comforting glow of a wood fire burning within.

Sighing with fatigue, Clorinda ordered the girl to place her chest on the floor and gave her sixpence. She was about to fling herself down upon the patchwork counterpane, when she caught sight of herself in a small mirror on the wall. Her face was white with the fatigue of the journey, her hair powdered with dust from the road, and her eyes looked hollow.

"The Duke certainly is not getting a beauty," she said aloud to her image. "I only hope he was not expecting one." Then smiling at the thought of his aristocratic dismay, she set to work to comb out the tangles and wipe away the dust. A little rosewater dabbed behind her ears, and a splash of cold water from a bowl on the chest of drawers was her toilet. Picking up her reticule, she determined to go in search of supper.

Clorinda was aware that an inn was no place for a gently-reared female, without even a servant to accompany her. As she hovered in the corridor, she noticed two men striding past the dining room. One was brown-haired and jolly looking: the other was older, perhaps thirty, and was dark haired. In him she recognized the demon driver whose gray horses had so imperiously swept by the stage coach. He was

23

laughing at something his companion had just said, but though his mouth was smiling, it seemed to partake at the same time of a cynical sneer.

"No, Marston," he said, as he brushed rudely past her, oblivious of her presence. "I fear there will be no Cyprians for us tonight. Just as well perhaps. I have not told you, but I am to be married on the morrow. It would be unsuitable to spend the night in debauchery."

"Married?" cried the other, as they entered into a room off the corridor. "Julian, this is a joke of yours."

Clorinda would have heard more of their conversation, for neither man had shut the door of the room they had entered, but a waiter came down the corridor.

"Pray be so good as to fetch me a supper in my chamber," said Clorinda timidly; then as the waiter paused she added, "A bowl of bread and milk will be all I require."

The man looked doubtful, but when Clorinda pressed a shilling from her small store into his hand he spoke. "We are very busy in the kitchens, Miss," he apologized. "If you should wait here for a moment, I could fetch it out for you."

He turned back toward the kitchens and Clorinda had no alternative but to wait. From the private parlor she could not help hearing more of the laughing conversation.

"A man must marry, after all," the dark man was saying. "The de Villiers are a fine family and what better than a countrified Miss to raise a family and cause me no trouble."

"But, Julian," his companion replied, "a countrified Miss for you? Why all the debutantes of this season would marry you, if you but smiled at them. So would their married sisters, come to that, if divorce was easy."

"My dear Marston," was all the reply he got, "I know this only too well. But I am determined on a wife with no *town* ideas in her head. The girl is well bred and has lived retired. That is enough for me. If she is tolerable to look at, why so much the better."

"You mean you are marrying a girl you have never seen? But, Julian, what will Lady Lancaster think?"

At this point the waiter reappeared bearing a tray with bread and milk upon it. Thanking him softly, Clorinda took it from him and returned to her lonely bedchamber.

Back in her room she ate her bread and milk thoughtfully. It seemed that this was the man to whom she was betrothed. She thought of that saturnine expression and shivered. She relived the moments when the powerful horses, galloping like beasts possessed, had swept by the coach. Well, he could pick his horseflesh at least, she thought. And he could drive like the devil, too.

Then she thought of how he had so carelessly walked by her, not sparing a glance for the poor dab of the female in the corridor. He and his friend had the arrogant bearing of men who had never spared a thought for ordinary people. Such arrogance was rather frightening. The friend at least had looked as if he might possess a heart, but the Duke . . . Again Clorinda shivered.

Somehow Clorinda had imagined that a Duke would be a dull and prosy bridegroom. She had pictured to herself a very formal gentleman with a taste for long words and ceremonials. It had never occurred to her that she might be marrying a man like the satanic driver. Dull and prosy, he certainly would not be, but would he be kind?

That night she lay in bed unable to sleep. She tried to imagine herself at the altar, going through the marriage vows with this dark and fearsome stranger. Somehow she could not imagine it. And what of the marriage after that—what would be expected of her? "Oh, Mama," her heart wailed, "you told me that gentlemen were different from females, but you did not tell me how. You always said I should marry for love, too. Why am I doing this?"

Then the image of gentle Emily came into her mind . . . and that of loving Robert Willoughby who had adored Emily from the age of six. She thought of him so young and proud in his love for her sister. It was for them, for their love, that she had come so far. After all, perhaps the dark stranger was not *her* Duke after all . . . On this reflection she eventually managed to sleep.

(2)

She woke with a start. Already the noise of grooms shouting at one another, inn servants bustling about, and the clatter of horses coming and going, was at full cry. It was later than she had thought. There was no time for her to dally now, no time for breakfast even. She leaped out of bed, scrambling to put her clothes together, and wishing that there was somebody to help her into the unbecoming pink frock. Then she took a hasty drink of cold water from the ewer on the chest of drawers, and ran a comb through her tangled locks. Weighed down with her leather chest, she rushed downstairs.

The stage coach was about to leave. There was just time for the coach driver to halt his horses. "Hurry my dear," shouted the jovial guard, "or we shall leave without you."

Even in the coach there seemed no time for reflection. In less than an hour they had arrived at the busy villages which made up the outskirts of London. To a country girl, all was astonishing. Peering out of the window, Clorinda was amazed at what she saw.

As they entered London, it seemed as if there

27

were people and coaches and carts and animals everywhere. The constant din of hundreds of people filled the air with the noise of cries, swearing, the screech of cart wheels, the rumble of carriages, and the clatter of iron-shod horses.

The coach then passed through a poorer area, and Clorinda was shocked to see the poverty and squalor all around her. Hoards of beggars, some big sturdy men, others poor cripples with wooden legs or stumps for arms, were everywhere. Ragged children ran in and out of the traffic.

But perhaps what shocked her most of all was the condition of the horses. At Villiers-sub-Arden, there had been many humble beasts, but for all that they were kept well and in good health—even the old nag that belonged to the rag and bone man. But here in London the poor beasts pulling the carts were often in a shocking condition. Their ribs stuck out with lack of feeding, while their sunken eyes and drooping heads showed how they had lost the natural high spirits of their kind.

The coach swept on through the traffic. Now the scenery changed. They were passing the houses of the rich in Mayfair. Neat maid servants were scurrying about the streets on errands, while footmen in multi-colored liveries and powdered hair passed them. Here and there Clorinda could see a man of fashion strolling to some rendezvous. Some wore the brightly colored coats and stretch-fitting pantaloons of the dandy, with high collar points and elaborate cravats at the throat.

The horses in this rich district were different too. They were all thoroughbreds, or glossy carriage beasts. Splendidly matched pairs pulled well-polished barouches in which sat fashionable ladies and their friends. Dandies dashed by, either in racing curricles or in phaetons. Even so Clorinda saw nothing to match the wonderful grays that had overtaken her coach the day before.

At the Golden Cross Inn where the stage coach finished its journey, she found an elegant equipage awaiting her with a coachman driving it and two footmen at the back. Inside was a fashionably dressed female of middle age. She wore an elaborately high bonnet with ostrich plumes, ruffled lace at the throat, and a kind of frogged redingote over a day dress.

She did not get out of the carriage to greet Clorinda but instead beckoned her inside. "I am the Duke's cousin, Lady Claremont," drawled the fashionable occupant. "I am to escort you to the church. But first you will no doubt want to change your clothes." She spoke abruptly, almost rudely. "No maid? Just the one chest?"

Clorinda nodded dumbly. The look she had given Clorinda's drab pelisse and faded pink gown made it clear that she considered her outrageously dowdy. Looking at Lady Claremont, Clorinda had the justice to see that she was quite correct.

Lady Claremont said nothing, as the elegant carriage journeyed through the streets. When the coach drew up at an imposing town residence the two ladies alighted. Passing through a large entrance hall and up a big staircase, Clorinda followed her modish guide who showed her into a bedroom. "Pluvier, my dresser, will wait on you," said Lady Claremont. She shut the door, leaving Clorinda alone with a thin-lipped, middle-aged woman who was obviously Lady Claremont's personal maid.

"Thank you," murmured Clorinda. "I fear I have

little in the way of clothes. If perhaps you could help me with my dress, I would be grateful."

Miss Pluvier was not to be won over by soft speech. It was evident that she resented this addition to her normal duties, and felt it was beneath her normal dignity to help such an underdressed female. Unsmilingly she helped Clorinda into the heavy gray silk dress that had been the only one of her Mama's which seemed suitable for a wedding.

"Madam has a tiara?" she queried.

"I have no jewelry at all," said Clorinda firmly. "But I have Mama's wedding veil."

From the chest she drew out a filmy creation of creamy lace. It was worked with such delicacy and devotion that it looked more like the handiwork of fairies than mere mortals. It was the same veil that her dear Mama had worn at her wedding to Sir Henry de Villiers, and that her grandmother had worn before her. Its graceful folds, according to family legend, had originated in Turkey where some adventurous Tudor ancestor had brought them back to delight the females of his family.

For the first time the ladies' maid nodded approvingly. "The veil is very nice, Madam, if I may say so," she said. "But might I venture a suggestion about your dress. Something in white might have been more appropriate."

"I have only a simple muslin in white," said Clorinda. "This will have to do."

After this exchange the haughty servant had said nothing, contenting herself with a mutter of disapproval as she brushed out the now faded and lifeless locks of Clorinda's once beautiful hair.

On her arrival at the church, Clorinda saw with relief that there were only about a dozen guests.

All of them had an air of astonished disdain upon their faces, when they were introduced to her.

Fortunately Jack de Villiers was there to support his sister. He strode forward to greet her with a hearty brotherly kiss. "Oh, Jack," whispered Clorinda, "I am so glad to see you."

"Now then, sister," chided her elder brother in a low voice, "you look more as if you're attending your funeral than your wedding. For goodness sake, try to smile."

"Has the Duke arrived?" she had whispered.

"Not yet, but he soon will be. Remember you must go through with it now. It's too late to change your mind. Try and *look* as if you wanted to marry him . . ."

There were a few dreadful minutes while she waited with Jack for the bridegroom to arrive. She could hear a hum of whispers rising from the pews, and the clergyman began to wear a worried look. "Curse him," her brother muttered, as he held her by the arm. "Is he going to run out?"

Then there was a sudden bustle and a tall figure strode into the church. It was he, the demonic aristocrat who had overtaken Clorinda's stage coach the day before. She could not mistake that sneering mouth, and those cold, bold eyes!

It was like a dream—no, a nightmare. It was with a sense of unreality Clorinda went through the marriage service . . .

When the clergyman finally gave a last blessing, Clorinda stole a glance at the tall impressive figure at her side. Throughout the service, the Duke had given his responses in a firm but emotionless voice. No feeling showed in his face, not even at the moment when he had placed the ring upon her finger, a moment marred by the fact that the ring, pure gold but curiously chased with an almost pagan pattern, had been too large.

Even now, thought Clorinda, she had to crook her third finger so that it would not fall off. Was it a bad omen? Did the Duke notice it? She could not tell. His eyes, his mouth, his whole bearing told nothing to the most attentive onlooker. There was no trace of any human reaction, except—and Clorinda found this hard to bear—a faint suspicion of boredom about his upper lip.

He was perfectly dressed, unlike his dowdy bride. He had chosen to array himself in the knee breeches which were the formal wear for court and great occasions. They were in black satin, and perfectly cut to his powerful thighs. His coat was so closely fitted that it must have taken all the exertions of a valet to shrug him into it.

A high collar and a snowy white stock arranged in intricate folds of a kind Clorinda had never seen before, completed his ensemble. At his embroidered waistcoat hung a quizzing glass. The only touch of jewelry about him was a heavy gold seal ring upon the fourth finger of his left hand.

As she walked down the aisle with this man who was a total stranger to her and to her family, Clorinda wondered whether it might not have been better for her—and for him, perhaps—if she had been left waiting at the church. She could not believe she was married.

This was not the wedding she had dreamed of, she thought, and a small sob rose in her throat. She choked it back, trying to think of Emily back at Villiers Manor. Emily at least would now have the kind of wedding the sisters had dreamed of—the flower-decked parish church, the friendly village parson, the respectful and well-wishing villagers, and their friends from the local gentry. Emily would walk down the aisle smiling with the thought of a lifetime of love ahead.

"I too must smile," thought Clorinda. "I must not let them see that I am miserable and frightened."

Tremulously she forced her lips into a constrained smile, and for a moment thought she noticed a flicker of approval in the eyes of a man at her side. "I am a de Villiers," she told herself, as the organ pealed out a triumphant march. "I will behave as my ancestors would expect me." Unconsciously she pulled back her shoulders to face the world.

It was a relief to discover a traveling carriage drawn up outside the church, with four chestnut horses champing at their bits. The phaeton with its grays by which the Duke had apparently arrived had disappeared, but the chestnuts were almost as splendid as their gray counterparts.

"I trust you will not be averse to spending your honeymoon at my estates in the country," said the Duke with impeccable politeness outside the church. "With such a quiet wedding as ours, a wedding breakfast seemed out of order. We can refresh ourselves on the road."

These were the first words he had addressed directly to her, for he had not bothered even to smile at the bride he had found awaiting him.

"It is quite all right, your Grace," Clorinda said with studied politeness. "You are too kind. I do not need any refreshment. Let us proceed as soon as possible. I am anxious to view my future home."

If her formality disconcerted him, he gave no sign of it. Instead, he helped her into the carriage and then followed her in. The four chestnut horses gave a mighty spring forward, as the groom at their heads leaped out of the way. The married pair were on their way.

To Clorinda's relief the Duke displayed none of the ardor that might have been expected from a newly-wed alone with his bride for the first time. He sat at the corner opposite her and did not even smile.

"You have some wonderful horses, Duke," she said, thinking that perhaps conversation was required of her.

"I am glad you think so." The Duke's dry response seemed to put an end to conversation. Clorinda abandoned her efforts to be polite.

The rest of the journey was undertaken in silence. From his corner the Duke said nothing, but instead lay back against the padded seat with eyes closed as if he was asleep. The rhythmical sounds of his breathing suggested this was more than just a pose.

Clorinda felt her indignation rising at his behavior. True, she wanted nothing less than kisses or lovemaking, but to sleep was surely carrying indifference too far. Not to be outdone, she too leaned back, closing her eyes. But sleep evaded her. Instead, she found herself wondering what sort of man her husband was. Would he demand her obedience, like the marriage service says a man may? Or would he keep up this dreadful indifference, demanding nothing, scarcely noticing her existence?

For the first time, she wondered if bleaching her hair had not been a mistake. Not only were the curling lively locks now lifeless and dull, but the perfect color of her complexion and the green of her eyes looked somehow wrong framed with insipid yellow. She was far from being a radiant bride.

Would the Duke have been so calmly sleeping in his corner, if he had been in the same chaise as the divinely blonde Emily, she wondered? Was he disappointed at the dowdy bride he had married? Then she remembered his cruelly cold words at the inn about a "countrified Miss who will raise my children and cause me no trouble."

The Duke has got what he deserves, she thought.

Her first glimpse of Westhampton diverted her mind from the man opposite her. As the fast chaise turned off the turnpike road, there stretched before it the rolling acres of English parkland. Huge oaks dating from Tudor times spread their branches. A herd of spotted fallow deer grazed beneath them as tamely as sheep.

At the lodge gates, the lodgekeeper and his wife and five children had turned out to bow and bob a curtsy at the passing carriage. The Duke had roused himself from slumber, and managed a casual wave at them. For the first time Clorinda began to realize some of the awesome responsibilities of the title she now shared. Naturally these people were eager to catch a glimpse of the girl the Duke had chosen. Their new Duchess was an important figure in their lives.

It had never occurred to her before that this wedding was more than a private thing. Suddenly she understood that it was like a stone cast into a pool. The ripples from the event would affect the lives of others, not just her own. She sighed. It was going to be more difficult than she had thought.

Past the lodge, the horses slowed down from a canter to a trot. Clorinda caught sight of the building that was to be her home. It was simply immense and very imposing.

All her life she had thought that Villiers Manor was the perfection of architecture. Its warm red brick and ancient wooden beams, its mullioned windows and rambling old rooms had been her ideal. What confronted her could not have been more different.

Westhampton had been built in the last century, when classical formality was all the rage. Its proportions were perfect, but on a gigantic scale. Stone columns rose impressively around a huge flight of steps to the massive double door. Large airy windows, quite unlike the higgledy piggledy windows of her childhood, seemed to glare from every part of its facade.

Everything about it was full of grandeur, formality and magnificence. It was indeed a country seat fit for a Duke, thought Clorinda with dismay, an aristocrat's imposing country establishment suitable for entertaining the top society of the fashionable world.

"That is Westhampton," said the Duke, and Clorinda could hear the pride in his voice. "Do you approve?"

"It is very, very big," was all she could manage. But if the Duke heard the note of terror in her voice, he did not deign to remark on it.

As the sweating chestnuts drew up in front of the front steps, Clorinda realized that a formidable welcome awaited her. A house steward, flanked by the butler and under-butler, came out of the double doors. Two footmen followed him, and ran down to open the carriage doors. Clorinda was daunted to see that all the household servants seemed to have been assembled within the entrance hall for her arrival.

"Good evening, Your Grace," the house steward bowed low. "I hope you had a pleasant journey. On behalf of all the household, I should like to offer their congratulations to your Grace and their best wishes to your new Duchess."

Weak with fatigue and overwrought with the emotions of the day, Clorinda swayed as she set foot on the ground. For a moment the scene swam dizzily in front of her eyes and she thought she would faint. But with a super-human effort she pulled herself up and began the slow progress up the steps.

In the entrance hall, the servants were lined up in order of precedence. Each curtseyed or bowed before her as the steward gave her their names. As well as the steward, the butler and the under-butler, there was a groom of the chambers, a valet, three footmen, a steward's footman, two oddmen, two pantry boys and a lamp boy. The women included eight housemaids, two sewing maids, two still room maids, six laundry maids, two kitchen maids, a vegetable maid, a scullery maid and one nursery maid. A French chef reigned in the kitchens.

At the end of the line, apart from the others, was a rather stout looking old lady with steel gray hair and spectacles. "Mrs. Scotney, the housekeeper," announced the steward.

"Good evening, Mrs. Scotney. I am happy to make your acquaintance and can see I shall need all your help with the household," said Clorinda. Thankfully she noticed there seemed real warmth in the older woman's smile despite her correctly formal curtsey.

"I expect Your Grace will be wanting to prepare for dinner," said Mrs. Scotney. "I will show you to the bedchamber."

As Clorinda followed her matronly figure up the huge stairway under the chandeliers that winked with what seemed a thousand candles, she had little chance to look around her. Though dusk was closing fast, the whole house seemed lit up. "The bill for wax candles, alone, must be enormous," thought Clorinda, remembering how the de Villiers household had tried to economize with these commodities.

She gained the impression of vastness—high ceilings wtih elaborate mouldings, formal portraits on the walls, costly velvet curtains and hangings. Westhampton was obviously maintained without consideration of cost. Jack must have been right. The Duke was as rich as Croesus.

It was the same in her bedroom—costly fabrics were everywhere. An immense four poster bed reigned in the middle of one wall. "Where does the door lead?" she asked Mrs. Scotney, pointing to a door in the opposite wall.

"That leads to His Grace's rooms," said the housekeeper.

Clorinda swallowed. They were to have connecting bedrooms then. "Was this the bedchamber of the last Duchess?" she asked.

There was a distinct pause before the housekeeper answered. "No, Your Grace," she said in an odd voice. "The last Duchess's rooms have been altered now. They are in the West wing which is rarely used save for guests at shooting parties."

As if anxious not to be questioned further, Mrs. Scotney then added, "You have no maid with you, Your Grace?"

"N . . . no," whispered Clorinda. It had never occurred to her that like other high born ladies she might be expected to bring her own ladies' maid with her to her new home.

"With your permission, Your Grace," the housekeeper suggested firmly, "I will send up Betty, one of the housemaids. She is a good girl, good with her needle and good in character."

Clorinda thanked her. With a warning that the Duke liked dinner to be served promptly on the hour, the stately Mrs. Scotney sailed out of the room, her household keys jangling at her waist and her stiff petticoats rustling with starch.

As she closed the door, Clorinda gave a low sigh. At last she was alone! She sank down at the dressing table and began to comb her hair.

With a despairing grimace, she looked down at the ugly gray dress she was still wearing. It looked quite out of place in these magnificent surroundings . . . yet her mother's pink day dress would look quite inappropriate for dinner. Having seen the fashionable Lady Claremont, Clorinda realized that all her mother's dresses were too long for the current fashion. All of them still had trains, which by now were obviously superseded

"There is nothing I can do for the present," she thought despairingly.

Dinner was a daunting occasion. The Duke and his new Duchess sat at opposite ends of a long walnut veneer table. Between them were several arrangements of flowers, and what seemed like an endless amount of silver. Behind each of their two chairs stood a footman with powdered hair, ready to supply their slightest want. A further flunkey stood at the side of the room, in readiness to bring in a seemingly endless succession of rich dishes.

Clorinda was bewildered. At Villiers Manor

the food had been good, but simple. She had never before been presented with such subtle sauces and so many gourmet dishes.

With each course came a different bottle of wine and a new rare vintage. It meant a wide selection of glasses of different designs in front of each place. Clorinda drank very little, taking only a sip from each glass. But she noticed that the Duke drained his dry, and that his footman refilled each glass more than once.

Drinking was the fashion of the day, she knew. The Prince Regent, later to become George IV, and his cronies thought it quite normal if after an evening party they were fit only for bed. A three-bottle man was quite ordinary. There existed also four, five and even six-bottle stalwarts.

Past the light of the candles glittering in their elaborately chased silver holders, Clorinda could see that the Duke was drinking heavily. She noticed that his eyes were sparkling and his cheeks were flushed.

But she could not talk to him. With the table stretching for what seemed miles between them, and the silver glittering in between, conversation was impossible.

Finally the Duke signaled for her to rise. "I will have my port in the library with the Duchess," he told the butler coldly. "Leave the decanter and one glass."

The library was paneled in wood, with matching leather volumes. They almost disguised the paneling, there were so many of them. It might have been a somber room but for a startlingly vivid portrait above the fireplace. The picture showed a lady in the formal dress of an earlier generation—wide skirts and a huge confection of powdered hair.

But it was the face that caught Clorinda's attention. It showed a woman laughing, yet somehow (Clorinda could not tell how she knew) tragically unhappy beneath the laugh. The dark eyebrows, high cheekbones and expressive black eyes denoted the close relationship between her and the present Duke.

Forgetting her constraint in his presence, Clorinda turned to the Duke and asked, "Who is the lady in the portrait?"

"It is my mother," he said curtly.

"She looks very like you," Clorinda remarked innocently.

The man in front of her said nothing. Instead he scowled. What had she said wrong? Looking at her husband sprawling on a leather armchair, caressing one of the sporting dogs that had somehow made their appearance, Clorinda made a mental note to be careful about what she said.

"I trust you will be happy here, Clorinda," said the Duke changing the conversation. It was the first time he had used her name since the marriage service, but there was no warmth in his voice. "Mrs. Scotney will no doubt show you around tomorrow. If you enjoy riding, you will find a lady's horse for you in the stables."

"Thank you, your Grace," said Clorinda formally. "I do enjoy riding. You are most generous. I hope I shall conduct myself as you would wish."

"Indeed I hope you will too," came the bored reply. "And now if you will excuse me, I must go and see to my chestnuts. I fancy the leader cut his fetlock as we turned past the lodge."

It was just an excuse, thought Clorinda angrily as she trod up the immense staircase toward her lonely bedroom. As if there were not grooms enough, and more, to look after the horses! Such a flimsy excuse to get rid of her made it obvious that the Duke had no wish to waste his time talking to his new bride! And yet he had suggested being together with her in the library.

Had that remark about his mother been so maladroit? It did not seem possible. He cares more for his chestnuts than for me, thought Clorinda with a little silent sob.

Later, as the fresh-faced housemaid, Betty, brushed her sad hair with soothing strokes, her common sense returned. What had she expected? Of course, the Duke cared more for his horses. He had probably chosen them himself, after inspecting their paces. Yet he had been content to order—and pay for, Clorinda thought bitterly—his bride without even seeing her.

"Your hair is so soft, Your Grace," the maid was saying, bobbing a little curtsey. "It is a pity it is so dry. Does Your Grace need anything more? Shall I help you into your nightgown?"

"No, thank you, Betty," replied Clorinda. She remembered that she must not show her unhappiness in front of this innocent bystander. "I think you have brushed my hair very nicely. As you say, it is a pity it is so dry. Perhaps you can help me get it into better condition."

The girl flushed with pleasure. Dropping a curtsey she went to the door. "We are so pleased to see a new mistress at Westhampton Hall," she said eagerly. "We all hope you will be very happy. Good night, Your Grace."

Smiling slightly at the thought of the young girl's naive good wishes, Clorinda slowly undressed herself, shrugging her slender body out of the heavy folds of the gray dress. Over her head she pulled the spotlessly white cotton nightgown that Emily had insisted she take with her.

Unlike her other clothes, it was wonderfully becoming. It had a yoke of exquisite embroidery set with tiny stitches by her mother in the last two years of her time as an invalid. A faint odor of rosewater still clung to it, a pure sweet smell that brought back, as nothing else could, the sights and sounds of Villiers Manor. For a second Clorinda imagined herself back there, in her small but neat bedchamber ...

She walked across from the bed back to the dressing table, and stared into the mirror there. From the glass an odd vision stared back at her. The white nightgown gave her a childish quality, which the gray silk dress had concealed. Its innocent material fell over her body in such a way as to outline the small girlish breasts, the slender flanks and the almost boyish form.

Her green eyes peered from a face that was pitifully white and drawn. But for the lank and unprepossessing yellow hair, it would have been a vision of a strange elfin beauty. As it was, Clorinda looked young, frail and far from well.

What do I do now? she wondered. She went back to the bed. It was larger than her simple couch at Villiers Manor. Much larger. The covers had been pulled down on either side for two people. Slowly and reluctantly she climbed into the left hand side.

She pulled the fleecy woolen blankets over her, burying herself deep into the linen sheets, so that only her elfin face protruded. It was if she was trying to hide herself under the rich coverlets.

Clorinda discovered that her heart was pounding with fear. She had thought Jack absurd, when he had said that day in Villiers Manor that she was too young for marriage. Now with a sickening race of her pulses, she realized he had been right all along. She was too young.

Nobody had told her what to expect. Her breathing seemed to come in uneven stops and starts. It was as if she could feel the blood moving round her body. Her mother had talked about gentlemen, she had mentioned their strange liking for the company of vulgar women like opera girls —but what had she really meant? Clorinda did not know—and the thought that she did not know made her unbearably frightened of what marriage involved.

She knew that a married man expected to sleep in the same bed as his wife. Would the Duke expect this too?

She could hear the library door bang down in the hall, and she sensed the footsteps of somebody coming up the front stairs. That firm but careless tread could only belong to the Duke! Was he coming to take his place at her side? If so, what should she do? Would he expect her to ... to kiss ... him?

Her heartbeats became more and more wild and rapid. Up and nearer came the steps. For a second it seemed they paused outside her door. Clorinda's heart seemed to halt altogether. They had proceeded down the corridor. She heard the door of an adjoining bedchamber open as he went in.

It occurred to her, more forcibly than ever before, that she must have been mad to have flung herself into this marriage. Though she had told Jack she knew what a marriage of convenience meant, she suddenly realized that that had been mere bravado. She knew what it meant in the eyes of the world, but what did it mean in the privacy of a bedroom?

"How foolish, how utterly and absolutely foolish I am," she reflected bitterly.

As she lay there, she thought she heard sounds from the adjoining room. Then they seemed to die down.

The Duke, so it seemed, required little from his bride. Although the coverlet on her bed had been turned down for two, he was not going to join her. Her heart's anxious beating slowed down, and her limbs stopped trembling. A wave of pure fatigue swept over her. As sleep came to her, she wondered why she should feel, among that great relief, a small pang of anger . . .

At breakfast the next morning, the new Duchess of Westhampton discovered that the Duke had already eaten and was out and about. "His Grace is trying out a new hunter," said the steward, in reply to her question. "Does Her Grace require to see to-day's menu?"

Clorinda shook her head. She had been quite a notable housewife, having run Villiers Manor ever since her mother had taken to her bed. But ordering a big country house, she knew, would be far more difficult. Understanding the complexities of footmen, ladies' maids, still rooms, French chefs, valets, under-butlers and so forth was not something she could immediately try to do. First she must get to know Mrs. Scotney, the housekeeper. She asked the steward to arrange for her to be taken round the house with this worthy.

Several exhausting hours later, after a tour of an unimaginable number of rooms, Clorinda sank on to a delicate sofa with a sigh of pure exhaustion. For a moment she closed her eyes . . .

"I hope Mrs. Scotney has not tired you out." The harsh voice brought her to her senses immediately. The Duke had entered. He was dressed in the casual riding breeches and highly polished riding boots that he had worn that night in the inn.

"Your Grace!" Clorinda struggled to her feet. She must speak to him. "I should be grateful for a moment of your time," she said.

"Pray be seated," was his courteous but somehow bleak reply. "I shall, of course, listen with attention to whatever you wish to say."

"Your Grace!" For a moment Clorinda could only repeat the phrase desperately. "I fear I shall need some new dresses," was what she next uttered. She looked down at her shabby pink gown. It was not what she had meant to start by discussing, but somehow it was uppermost in her mind.

"What woman does not?" said the Duke lightly. It should have been an agreeable remark, but Clorinda thought it sounded cynical. "I have arranged for you to be paid a monthly dress allowance," he continued. "You will not find me ungenerous, I think."

"Thank you." She forced herself to say the words in a meek tone. Whatever she did now, she must not antagonize him—for Emily and for Jack's sake, she must continue. "I do not know how much you know about the de Villiers family," she went on painfully. "We are not rich, and it was absolutely necessary that I should marry you. It was either me or my sister."

"Your sister?" For the first time, the Duke looked as if his attention had been held.

"I have an elder sister, Emily, who is engaged to

marry Robert Willoughby. He is the younger son of the Squire . . ." Clorinda could feel her voice faltering. "That is why . . . we decided I should go to London to marry you, not her. We forged Mama's signature on the letter," she carried on, determined to make a clean breast of the deception. "Mama is dead. She died the week before you wrote . . ."

"Go on," the Duke said grimly. "So I have married the younger sister, have I? I thought you looked scarcely out of the schoolroom. I have done this Robert Willoughby a good turn, it seems."

"I didn't think it would matter," said Clorinda in a small voice. "After all, you only cared about the de Villiers blood. It is true my sister is beautiful, which I am not. But you did not bother, or seem to care, about which sister you married."

"So I have missed the family beauty, have I?" the Duke said with a cynical smile. "Well, I do not seek for beauty in a wife. What is it that I can do for you?" I presume you have not confessed for nothing."

"I had hoped . . . that you might be able . . . to do something to help Robert Willoughby," said Clorinda doubtfully. "He is only a younger son, and he needs a patron. And then there is my brother Jack. I am afraid he has dreadful debts . . ."

"That is no news," observed the Duke. "I am only surprised that your brother has escaped a debtors' prison for so long if he must gamble with a bad set like Lord Winterstoke's. You should tell him he can only lose with such companions."

"I fear he will not listen to me," said Clorinda. "I had hoped you might do something for him, now you are married to a de Villiers."

"They speak the truth when they say it is just a

matter of price with all women," said the Duke unpleasantly. "The de Villiers alliance comes expensive, I see." He paused. Clorinda longed to stand up and tell him that she did not want his money. But she forced herself to remain silent. "I shall pay up, Madam wife," he observed with a curl of the lip.

"In return, I shall try to be the kind of wife you would like," was all that Clorinda could think to say. "I shall do my duty."

"I trust you will," was the Duke's dry reply. "I did not marry a chit from the country to have her setting up her will against mine."

With these words, he turned on his heel. As he opened the door to leave, he said harshly, "I am returning to London. I have some urgent business. I trust you will find adequate employment here."

"How long will you be gone?" said Clorinda timidly.

"My household are trained to expect me at any time," he said, still with a sneer about his mouth. "As my wife, I expect you to follow their example."

(3)

Alone in the immense house, Clorinda imperceptibly began to feel a little happier. She was lonely, of course, but there was something soothing, even healing, about her solitary state. The noble history of the house, its having belonged to so many generations of Westhamptons before her, was calming.

Others had loved and suffered there, she felt. Often she would go into the library and gaze at the picture of the last Duchess. The portrait somehow seemed to express sympathy for her plight—as if her predecessor had known what it was like to be unloved. It seemed to say: "You will carry on the Westhampton tradition. Be strong. Do not be fainthearted."

Besides the many treasures in the house, there was a delightful little Arab mare waiting for Clorinda in the stables. "She's a proper handful," the head groom warned, "but there's not an ounce of vice in her." The mare looked out of her stable and whinnied gently. When Clorinda offered her an apple she had brought down to the stables, she bowed her graceful head and blew gently into Clorinda's outstretched hand.

Mrs. Scotney solved a problem that confronted Clorinda. She had no proper riding habit. Her shabby old habit from Villiers Manor she had deemed too old to bring with her. She wanted to ride. She had always been an enthusiastic horsewoman, but she must find something to wear.

"Your Grace is in need of a riding habit?" asked Mrs. Scotney kindly. "I know that the Duke would like you to ride. He is a neck and nothing rider, himself, and I am sure he would approve of you taking this exercise."

Clorinda did not like to say that she thought the Duke would probably not care either way what his wife did. So instead she merely asked, "Can I get one made in the village?"

"There is a village dressmaker," said Mrs. Scotney doubtfully, "but I do not think she could manage a riding habit. If I may venture my opinion, what you need is something tailored in London."

Clorinda sighed. "No doubt, you're right. But I cannot go to London yet, and in the meantime that means I cannot ride."

"Perhaps I can help you," said the housekeeper slowly. With these words she bustled out of the room, coming back shortly with a magnificent, if out of date, green velvet costume. "It's old fashioned, Your Grace," she warned, "but I think it will fit you."

When Clorinda tried it, it fitted perfectly. She swept down the stairs holding its train, and went to show herself to Mrs. Scotney. "You look quite beautiful," said the old woman. "She was beautiful too."

"Who was beautiful?" Clorinda asked.

"Why, the lady whose costume you are wearing." Something in the housekeeper's voice was wary.

"Tell me who she was." Clorinda spoke softly.

Mrs. Scotney looked round the empty hallway. "It belonged to the last Duchess," she said, "she whose portrait is in the library. When she left, she would not take any of her clothes. Ball gowns, riding costumes, furs, day dresses, even her night gowns, she left them all behind. She was too proud to take anything. God forgive her."

The tale mystified Clorinda. Ushering the guilty-looking housekeeper into the blue salon, she confronted her and demanded, "Surely the Duke's mother is dead now? How did she leave and why?"

Mrs. Scotney looked distressed. "It is not my place to tell you, Your Grace. I had thought you must have known. The whole world knew about it. The scandal could not be hushed up."

"I have lived retired in the country," Clorinda said quietly. "Papa took no interest in the doings of the fashionable world, and I know very little about it. But I think I ought to know about the family into which I have married. It might make things easier for me with . . ."

Here she broke off. She was going to say "make things easier for me with the Duke." Then she thought perhaps she should not discuss him with his household.

But Mrs. Scotney seemed to sense what she meant. "He was such a loving and affectionate boy," she said sadly, and both women knew about whom she was talking. "When the Duchess left, it broke his heart. He was so open, so eager—and so vulnerable.

"The Duchess had never been happy you see. The late Duke, well, it was true he was nothing less than a rake. He ignored her. It wasn't so much the other women that hurt her, as the lack of affection he showed toward her. She was a lady who needed love like a flower needs the sunlight.

"Then eventually she left. She had pined for years . . . then a Marquis came over here from Paris. Well, it all ended with her leaving Westhampton forever. They tell me she was happy for a brief time in France even though she had all those foreigners around her."

"What happened to her?" Clorinda breathed.

"She died in childbirth, some say. But none of us knew for sure. The French revolution occurred within a year or two and nobody knew what happened to the Marquis or to her. The old Duke would not have her name mentioned in the house, not for anything.

"Master Julian, the Duke I should say, was too young to understand it all, but it's my belief that it left its mark. That's why we were all so glad to hear that he had got married at last. But I must not stay chattering here," went on the housekeeper. "You'll be discreet, Your Grace? I shouldn't really have talked so freely but, if you didn't know, perhaps it was best I should tell you."

"I'll be discreet," promised Clorinda. She had realized that the housekeeper meant well. Nobody was more loyal to the Westhampton family than Mrs. Scotney. At first Clorinda had thought this would mean that she might dislike the schoolgirlish bride thrust in their midst. But now she understood.

If Mrs. Scotney had thought it was odd that the Duke should desert his young bride so soon after his wedding, she had made no comment on it. Instead, she seemed to assume that Clorinda, like herself, would be happy to wait here at Westhampton at the Duke's pleasure.

The riding habit was a boon. Now Clorinda could spent happy hours exploring the spacious grounds—with a groom following a respectful distance behind of course.

She had begun to be accustomed to the formality that surrounded her—the scores of servants, the ceremony at every meal, and the strict hierarchy of the servant's hall. She had discovered that despite this, there was considerable affection displayed toward the Duke.

Whatever he might be in the outside world, by his household he was respected and (this she found strange) loved. Yes, loved was the only word for it. His Grace's wishes, his probable desires, his tastes, his interests and his well-being were the focus of all that vast organization that revolved round Westhampton.

As she cantered along the turn of the deer park upon the little Arab mare, which Clorinda had named Firefly, she felt a pang of pity for the Duke. He must have been a sad little boy, abandoned by his Mama, forbidden to mention her name, and with a rakish father who no doubt spent most of his time in London rather than with his heir in the country. Was this the secret of the Duke's distrust of women? Was this why he had chosen a wife from the country without ever seeing her? Was this the key to his arrogance? She remembered that he had said at the inn that he had chosen a wife from the country who would "cause no trouble." Did he fear that his Duchess might leave him in the same way that his mother had left his father?

She was torn between exasperation and pity. Pity because of the small boy's sufferings that had made the adult man so cold. Exasperation, because she was the dowdy wife left in the country.

As golden summer day followed golden day, slowly Clorinda was no longer the dowdy wife she had first been. The dry yellow locks which she had so foolishly bleached began to grow out. "Your Grace's hair needs proper attention," Betty had said worriedly one night, contemplating the tell-tale signs of red-gold at the roots.

"Can you keep a secret, Betty?" breathed Clorinda.

"Oh yes, Your Grace. You know I would do anything for you, Your Grace," said the eager girl.

"My hair used to be red. I bleached it blonde. But now I would its natural color to grow again."

"I think I could cut it short, your Grace," said Betty. "Short curls are more fashionable today than long hair anyway."

To Clorinda's affectionate amusement the young maid entered into the spirit of the thing. She produced herbal washes which she said would start the process of making the bleached hair go back to its natural color. At the same time she encouraged Clorinda to wear a large shady sun hat, so that the transformation could be produced little by little without too much notice from the household staff.

After several days, the red gold curls were clearly visible, and as Betty snipped off the dam-

54

aged bleached hair, Clorinda began to look her old self.

True, her hair was no longer the magnificent red waving mane of old. But in its stead was a short, tightly curled mass of red. "Like a halo, your Grace," breathed the adoring Betty.

And truly the radiant locks did have something otherworldly about them—something perhaps more of the fairy than the angelic world.

Clorinda was relieved. Anything was better than the lifeless yellow hair that had made her look so faded and washed out. Her spirits began to rise.

Her new found happiness was increased by a letter from her sister Emily. When it arrived, she realized in her worry about the Duke and her obsession with her new life, she had all but forgotten that her sister must soon be wedded to Robert Willoughby. Eagerly she tore open the paper.

Dearest sister, she read, *I have been wed in haste since your Departure, the Squire thinking that a marriage was best in case creditors besieged the Manor. My husband, darling Robert, says that I should tell you he is your eternal debtor, since you were the means to our union.*

"We have since met the Duke in London, whither we repaired for our honeymoon. He paid a visit to us and promised to be a Patron to Robert. Indeed, he has found Robert a post at Admiralty House, and we are now settled in London where I trust we may soon encounter you.

"I beg of you a letter, since I am persuaded your Happiness in your marriage must all be equal *to mine. The Duke is a little stiff it is true, but a man of great Generosity . . .*

There followed news of Villiers Manor, and a note added by the young bridegroom wishing his "dear sister" happiness and giving heartfelt thanks for the intervention of the Duke. It added: "The Duke has paid Jack's debts too. We are deeply obliged to him."

"Well," thought Clorinda, "he has done as he promised. Yet he might have told me himself, instead of leaving my sister to give the good news." Again she wondered at her irritation with the Duke. Surely he had done all that she wanted? A marriage without any ties was what she had envisaged, and it seemed it was what she had got. Her family was now looked after. Jack's debts were settled. Emily and Robert could be happy.

"But I am the one who has had to pay," she thought angrily. "I have been left here like an old glove, cast aside as if fit only for the country, while the Duke enjoys himself in town."

The next day brought a brief missive from Jack confirming the Duke's settlement of his debts. "The Duke has paid up handsomely," it read saucily. "Mind you do your side and be a good wife. He is not one to Trifle with, I fancy. Your loving brother etc."

Clorinda pondered over both letters. By now Emily as well as Jack would be in London, enjoying the fashionable life. "Why, they have both seen more of the Duke than I," she thought. "I have to wait here till he deigns to visit me. They must meet him nightly at parties, and ridottos, and balls and all manner of routs."

She employed one morning writing a letter to the Duke. It was more difficult than she thought but after wasting several sheets of paper, she managed a note that while friendly seemed to have the requisite air of formality. In it, she requested his permission to join him in London.

If she had expected a reply, the response surprised her. For two days there was no letter. Then on the third the steward came to her and said, "Your Grace, His Grace the Duke has asked me to inform you that he wishes you to stay at Westhampton until it is more convenient for him to return."

"Where is his letter?" asked Clorinda. She tried not to let the steward see her anger. She had been trained not to display emotion in front of servants.

"There is no letter, Your Grace," the man said respectfully. "His Grace sent a message with one of the grooms together with some papers about the estate. If the message is unclear, I can send for a man for you to question him."

Clorinda looked suspiciously at him. Was he aware of her fury? His face seemed as normal as usual, serious and anxious to please. "No," she said decidedly. "His Grace is quite correct. I should prefer to stay here for the present anyway."

The refusal of her request spurred her to action. She ordered a chaise, drove to the village, and asked the village dressmaker to make her two day dresses at high speed. It could be done, she learned, in three days' time. The dresses would not be in high fashion, but at least they would be less dowdy than the ones of her mother that she was still having to wear.

After she had done this, she felt slightly better. Then an extraordinary idea began to grow in her mind. She would teach the Duke a lesson. She would show him that he could not keep her, like some poor dependant or like a dog, in the country, treated with less affection than his horses. She *would* go to London, after all, but she would not tell him about her journey.

"After all," she argued to the picture of the last Duchess in the library, "he has not treated me well. He obviously thinks I am not worth bothering about. Well, I shall show him that I am. I will go to London and I will go disguised. I shall make the Duke fall hopelessly and madly and passionately in love with me, and I shall be positively heartless to him in return."

Surely he would not recognize that dowdy figure in the flame-red haired girl she had since become? Her hair was cut short, when before it had been long. Its color was entirely different.

"I shall need new clothes, of course," she thought. "And I must get my hair cut properly. I will need lots of clothes, since the ones I am getting done in the village will only do to arrive in. I must not be seen in anything but the latest and more exotic fashions."

She could count on the support of Emily and Robert. Even if they did not approve they could hardly fail to help the sister who had made their own marriage possible. Jack, too, must be commanded to help. He would not like it, Clorinda knew, but he had never been one to desert his family when they were in a scrape.

"He will have to help," she said to herself. "Otherwise I shall tell him that I will ask the Duke not to help him again with money." It was obvious to even Clorinda that Jack was a confirmed gambler. Though the Duke had paid his debts this once, Clorinda felt sure that by now Jack had probably run up more.

"I shall need a pseudonym," she thought. "I had better stick to my own initials. De Vere would do for a surname, and perhaps something like Cecilia for a christian name. And I shall pretend I am a schoolfriend of Emily's, who has been very close to the whole family. That way, nobody will be surprised at my intimacy with Jack."

The more she thought about it, the more she liked the idea. It was complicated, to be sure. It might not work. But at least it would get her into the world of fashion. Clorinda admitted to herself that she longed for a little gaiety, a party or two, the sights of London, the pleasures of being part of the haute monde of high society. It seemed unfair that her brother and sister might enjoy these at their leisure while she had been left in the country.

That night she lay in her sumptuous four-poster bed planning it all carefully. It was important, she thought, to think things out. Nothing would be worse than to embark on a course of action that failed—and left her worse off than before.

She would tell Mrs. Scotney that she had to return to Villiers Manor urgently, because of an unexpected illness of her sister. The housekeeper would probably expect her to go to nurse a beloved sister. But then Clorinda realized that Mrs. Scotney would probably suggest taking the Duke's second traveling coach.

That might ruin all. She would have to travel by stage coach. Somehow she must persuade Mrs. Scotney that this was all right. Then came the problem of having an escort. The obscure Clorinda de Villiers might travel alone up to London but this would never do for the Duchess of Westhampton. Such conduct would be looked on as either deplorably fast or unforgivably eccentric.

She had a shrewd idea that Mrs. Scotney might enlist the support of the Duke to stop her doing that. The only answer seemed to have Betty's help. "Can I trust Betty?" she wondered. The girl *seemed* fond of her. "I must ask her tomorrow . . ." was her last thought before she drifted off to sleep.

✻　✻　✻

The next day things turned out more easily than she had envisaged. Her plan worked perfectly. Mrs. Scotney was quite unsuspicious. Indeed, she was full of sympathy about the pretended illness of her sister, and offered to send a hamper of comforts like arrow-root, calf's foot jelly, and lemons. When Clorinda explained that she could hardly travel by stage coach burdened with these delicacies, Mrs. Scotney was shocked.

"I should think not, Your Grace. Surely you will be ordering Peter the under-coachman to take the second traveling coach?"

"I would prefer to go to by stage—with Betty to accompany me, of course."

"His Grace would wish you to travel in his own carriage," said the housekeeper firmly but deferentially. Clorinda had the impression that she was trying to be kind in pointing this out.

She decided to risk all by appealing to her sympathetic nature. "I know that," she said slowly, "but, you see, Mrs. Scotney, I come from a proud family. The de Villiers are proud but we are not rich. I should not like my sister to feel I was showing off my new and wealthy position, by arriving in a private carriage. I would do anything rather than show up her relative poverty."

"Well, Your Grace, I honor your feelings," said Mrs. Scotney. "But I don't know what His Grace would say, to be sure."

"I shall not trouble him with this," said Clorinda. "But I will return by the carriage probably." On this note of compromise the conversation ended. Clorinda was fairly sure that Mrs. Scotney would not complain to the Duke now. "As if he would care, anyway . . ." she said to herself.

Letting Betty into the secret went equally smoothly. The young girl had accepted her new job as Clorinda's maid with understandable enthusiasm. From housemaid to personal maid was a definite step up the career ladder for any servant, and she had agreed with Mrs. Scotney's remark that it was "the chance of a lifetime, Betty—so mind you do your best."

Of course she had been thrilled. She knew that if she gave satisfaction, she might retain the post. So she determined to do her best, however difficult and demanding this new Duchess might be.

In fact Clorinda was the perfect mistress. As soon as the village dressmaker had completed a couple of tolerable day dresses, Clorinda had passed on to Betty the gray dress in which she had been married and the pink dress that had been worn by her Mama.

It was not just this generosity that had endeared her to the young maid. Clorinda's gentle ways, her kindness to her inferiors, and her unvarying courtesy to even the lowest in the land, had won Betty's un-swerving allegiance. She idolized her soft-spoken mistress for her own sake, not for her rank.

That evening when Betty was brushing her now glorious hair with the hundred strokes she always gave it, Clorinda asked her, "Can I trust you, Betty? Would you do something special for me? Could you keep a secret, with your life, if need be?"

"I'd do anything for you, Your Grace," said the girl eagerly. "Anything at all. You have been so kind to me. I never thought that I would find such a mistress."

"I hardly know how to explain this, Betty . . ." Clorinda went on painfully. Though she was hardly older than the maid, she felt difficulty in revealing the truth. "The Duke does not love me. He never did. Our marriage has never been . . . a proper marriage. There is no love between us.

"So I have decided to go up to London and see if I can win the Duke's love," she went on, "as it does not look as if he is going to return here very often. He thinks of me as a young and badly dressed girl, with horrid yellow hair. If I go to London, and buy fashionable dresses, perhaps I can touch his heart . . ."

"Oh, Your Grace . . ." the girl breathed.

"But it must be a secret, so secret that nobody knows of it save you and I. You see, Betty, I am going to pretend to be somebody else—a Miss de Vere that the Duke has never met before. That way he will meet me anew. He will not recognize me through the deception. He has never bothered to pay me any attention. I doubt if he gave his wife a second glance . . ." Here Clorinda broke into a sob.

She pulled herself together. "If he knew who I

was he would probably just send me back to West-hampton. But if he meets me as a stranger, perhaps . . . perhaps he will fall in love."

There was silence. Betty's eyes were wide with sympathetic amazement and admiration. Clorinda's were suffused with tears.

"There is another reason why I do not want anybody to know what I am doing or where I am going. If I fail . . . if I fail . . . .then I must come back here and learn to be a dowdy wife who lives in the country, bears children, and rarely sees her husband. It will be less painful if nobody knows that I had tried to win his regard."

"You won't fail," Betty burst in, mindless of the convention that a servant should not interrupt her employers. "You are so beautiful now. Any man would fall in love with you, I think."

Clorinda smiled tremulously. The loyalty and affection she had inspired was enormously heartening. She looked into the mirror reflectively. "I wonder if the Duke likes red hair," she mused aloud. "I am sure that my eyes are not a fashionable color. Whoever heard of a lady of fashion with red hair and green eyes?"

*   *   *

The next day she set out with an excited Betty in attendance. This time she traveled in great luxury. Instead of the poor little leather chest with which she had arrived, she had the imposing luggage of the Westhampton family, and a purse full of golden guineas supplied by the steward who doled out her allowance.

It was easy enough to change direction after the

stage coach's first stop at a big town. Instead of going south to Villiers Manor, she turned North to London, changing coaches.

This time the journey was less adventurous and more impressive. The possession of money, awarded to the various inn servants and coachmen, made the experience smooth. Betty unconsciously seemed to know how to handle this kind of thing, and succeeded in making it clear that her mistress was used to both luxury and respect. Money and a servant, it seemed, shed a special protection on one, thought Clorinda.

When they arrived in London, therefore, there was no difficulty in finding a hackney carriage to convey them to the small house in Mayfair where her sister was now living. It was not one of the houses of the most fashionable rich, but it nevertheless had an unmistakable air of gentility.

It was a weary young Duchess, nonetheless, who arrived at her sister's home. As the servant showed her into a small but neat drawing room, Emily greeted her with a cry of joy. The two sisters flung themselves into each others' arms, laughing and half crying with pleasure. It was the first affectionate gesture that Clorinda had received since she had left Villiers Manor so many days ago—it seemed like years to Clorinda since that farewell.

She stood back from her sister holding her at arms' length, for a moment surveying her. Emily blushed slightly. Her eyes were soft with happiness, and her complexion perfect with pink and white. "Marriage agrees with you, dearest Emily," said Clorinda a trifle wistfully.

Just then Robert Willoughby strode in. He

wrung her hand with a manly grasp, then kissed her warmly on the cheek. "Dearest sister," he said with strong emotion. "I cannot tell you of my gratitude. It is marvelous to see you. But where is the Duke? Does he expect you?"

Clorinda cleared her throat nervously. "Can I ask you to see that my maid Betty is looked after?" she said a trifle irrelevantly. "I do not know where the Duke is, Robert. He does not know I have come to London."

Seeing that her sister was tired and over-wrought, Emily helped her to a chair, taking her pelisse and ordering the butler to look after Betty. "We will drink a glass of ratafia together," she said quietly. "You shall tell us all about it, Clorinda. You know Robert and I would do anything to help you."

The sweet liqueur, flavored with almonds, peach and cherry kernels, revived Clorinda, and she found herself explaining everything to Emily and Robert —the Duke's indifference, his return to London, his refusal to let her join him, and her decision to go anyway.

"We knew the Duke was in town, of course," said Emily, "but I thought perhaps you had pre-ferred to stay down in the country. It is said to be a wonderful estate. But will he not be angry, Clorinda, that you have disobeyed him and come to town?"

To gentle Emily the thought of disobeying a husband was obviously terrible. Clorinda could see that her happiness with Robert was so overwhelming that Emily could not understand the indifference— nay, the bitterness—that she felt towards her ducal husband.

"He will not know that I am here," she said

65

with spirit. "I have a plan, Emily." She outlined her scheme to take a false name and to pretend to be a schoolfriend, rather than the sister, of Emily.

"He has only seen me as a dowdy girl, and that is how he thinks of me still, I am sure. But when I am dressed properly, and now that my hair is almost as it used to be, then perhaps he will at last notice that I am not so ugly." She blushed a little, and looked appealingly at Robert. "My plan is to make the Duke fall in love with me, not knowing who I am."

"Oooh Clorinda, you do have good ideas. How is it you always seem to think up a plan? Don't you remember how Mama said you had a wise head on young shoulders." Emily was enthusiastic. Her eyes glowed. It was obvious that once again she thought her younger sister wonderfully ingenious.

Turning to her husband she asked, "Don't you think it's a good idea? It must be perfectly miserable for Clorinda left alone in the country, never seeing the Duke. Perhaps this way she can make her marriage work and become as happy as ours."

Her words made Clorinda feel guilty. She knew in her heart of hearts that her motives were not so good as Emily thought. The Duke had bitterly hurt her pride. She had not expected romantic love from him; but nor had she expected such a total and absolute indifference. Clorinda wanted to make him love her and love her so deeply that it hurt.

Robert was doubtful about the plan at first. "We shall support you, of course, Clorinda. I can do no less after all that you have done for both of us. But what will you do if the Duke doesn't fall in love? Or, come to that, what will you do if he *does*?"

"I am sure it will all turn out all right somehow," said Clorinda vaguely. "You must admit, Robert, that

I do anyway badly need some clothes. Who would think that I was married to one of the richest men in England?" She made a little grimace of disgust, gesturing to the plain daydress she was wearing. It was serviceable, but clearly the work of the village dressmaker. Emily could see that. Even Robert as he looked at it noticed that it was not in the height of fashion.

"If the worst comes to the worst," Clorinda added, "at least I shall have spent some time in London. I shall have been to some parties, before I am buried in the country forever. You must understand."

"I am sure the Duke will not be able to resist you, once you have some new clothes," put in Emily warmly. "Your hair looks much better already. It was a shame for us to bleach it. But perhaps it was just as well—the Duke might have wondered if a red-haired de Villiers had turned up at the church. It is odd how different you look now that the bleach has worn off."

The next morning Jack called on his sisters—after Robert had sent him an urgent message. He found both of them in Emily's boudoir poring over fashion plates in a lady's periodical. "I am sure you would look perfectly ravishing in this design," Emily was saying to her younger sister, pointing at a very elongated lady wearing an extremely modish gown.

"I am sure she will," said Jack, "but she ought not to be here. It's not the thing for a bride to go jaunting off on her own, disobeying her husband, and leaving him just like that."

His words brought both girls to their feet in an instant. Clorinda ran across the room helter skelter, throwing herself into his fraternal embrace. "Don't be severe, Jack," she said coaxingly. "Besides I haven't left the Duke. He left me first."

Jack grinned. "Well then, my romp of a younger sister," he laughed, "have you cut loose already? Robert tells me you have some plaguey complicated scheme to make the Duke fall in love with you. Sounds like a romance out of a book to me."

"It's a marvelous plan, Jack," Clorinda pleaded. "You've got to help me. I shall need you to teach me to dance and to escort me to all the town parties—with Emily to chaperone me, of course, and with Robert too."

"Doesn't sound as if you need me at all," said her brother firmly. "Going to high society parties is not my line at all. I'm more at home in a snug little club with a roulette wheel, myself."

"No, I must have you too, Jack," said Clorinda. "It's essential to my plan. It has got to look as if I have plenty of admirers and you can be one of them. After all, I did get the Duke to pay off those debts of yours. You wouldn't be so unhandsome as to let me down, now, would you?" She ended on rather a pathetic note.

Jack de Villiers was a scapegrace and a gambler, but he was not a man to let down his friends or family. "Honor of a de Villier," he said good-naturedly. "I'll help. Mind you, I'd lief as not have to go to a lot of routs and balls with you when I might be handling the dice with dandies like Winterstoke. What do you want me to do this morning, though? You can't go anywhere dressed as you are."

"I'm glad you understand," said Clorinda briskly. "The first stage in my plan of campaign is to buy lots of clothes. The Duke will never give me a second glance unless I am dressed in the height of fashion. I have lots of money with me, and what I need to know now is the best dressmaker in the whole of London. Can you tell me who that is?"

Jack thought for a moment. "Mademoiselle Fanny—no, she's too *ingenue*. I take it, sister," he said, "that you want something that is elegant and a little unusual?"

"That's right."

"Mrs. Berkeley is too fussy . . . I know," he ejaculated suddenly. "You must go to Madame Genevieve Latour. There's a look about a Genevieve dress that everybody admires."

"Is she really the best?"

"She's so good that she dresses Lady Lancaster, and after all, Clorinda, that makes her the dressmaker you ought to have if you are trying to attract the Duke."

Lady Lancaster? The name seemed somehow familiar. "What do you mean?" asked his sister. "Who is Lady Lancaster, and what does she have to do with me trying to attract the Duke?"

"Oh Lord," groaned her brother, "I should not have mentioned that. Forget it, Clorinda. The Duke would half kill me if he discovered I had mentioned that lady to you."

Then seeing from a mulish look on her face that she was about to ask more questions, he added, "Now be a good girl. There's nothing in it any more, I dare say."

This last remark mystified Clorinda even more. "What on earth do you mean, Jack? Nothing in what? Do you mean that the Duke admires Lady Lancaster?"

"Yes, that's it. Now I am not going to say anything more about it. Men are men after all, Clorinda, and you told me yourself that you understood what a marriage of convenience meant."

"All right," said his sister submissively. She did not like to confess that she still did not understand. She remembered her mother saying that men sometimes had their opera dancers as friends after their marriage. "Mama had said that a lady pretends she does not know about them," thought Clorinda.

Yet her Mama had never mentioned friendships with women in high society. She had understood about the opera dancer, she thought. It was probably just the same kind of friendship that men had with stud grooms, cockfighting experts, boxers and all the other sports that they so much enjoyed. But why should there be anything special about a friendship with a high born lady?

"You mean that Lady Lancaster is a sort of rival of mine?" she said to Jack. "I won't ask you to tell any more, but is that why you thought I ought to go to Madame Genevieve?"

"That is it," said Jack uncomfortably.

She did not bring up the subject again with him. But she could not help remembering the conversation she had overheard in the inn, when the Duke had told his friend that he was getting married.

"But, Julian, what will Lady Lancaster think?" had been his friend's comment. Clorinda had not been able to hear the Duke's reply. What did it all mean?

(4)

The establishment of Madame Genevieve Latour was discreetly situated just off one of the crowded shopping areas of Mayfair. There was nothing about the elegant Georgian house to betray the fact that its owner was a couturier—unless it was the stream of elegantly dressed fashionable women going in and out.

For Madame Latour was not an ordinary dressmaker. Her couture establishment was so well known, and so very fashionable, that she could pick and choose her customers. It was rumored that she had once refused to dress a Countess on the grounds that this lady's ample form would not do her gowns justice.

For Emily and Clorinda waiting upon the steps of the Latour fashion house, it was a surprise to see the door opened by a smartly dressed footman. The illusion of being in a private house was continued, when the two girls somewhat nervously clutching their reticules, were shown into a well-furnished room like any lady's drawing room.

The woman who was there to greet them was, as might be expected, perfectly gowned in a well-cut,

71

extremely simple, almost severe day dress cut high at the neck. The frock conveyed elegance and refinement rather than showiness.

Madame Latour had a serious face with strong features, dark hair, and large eyes. She was in her late thirties, Clorinda guessed—or perhaps a little older. Most surprising of all, however, was that here was indubitably a lady rather than a tradeswoman.

Coolly she introduced herself in a low voice with just a trace of a French accent. She asked what she could do for them in a way that made it seem as if she was their hostess, rather than any connection with the commercial world.

Clorinda was too astonished to say anything, but Emily said haltingly, "I am Mrs. Willoughby, and this is a schoolfriend of mine making her debut in London. She has just arrived from the country, and, as you can see, she needs some clothes."

There was an imperceptible rising of the eyebrows on behalf of the French woman. She contemplated the two girls before her. Emily was simply, though elegantly dressed—thanks to the Squire's generosity in the matter of her wedding and trousseau. Clorinda on the other hand, was wearing a dress made up hurriedly by the Westhampton dressmaker. Under the expert scrutiny of Madame Latour, she felt, as never before, that she had no pretensions to elegance or beauty.

But whatever Madame Latour may have thought about the village fashions, she did not say it. Instead she merely asked, "Forgive me for saying this, but are you aware that my modes are *tres chère*, exceedingly expensive?"

"I know that." Clorinda spoke slowly. "But it is not just gowns that I want. I want to become a new woman—nothing less than the most beautiful woman in London. I know that only you can do this for me. For that, I would willingly pay a small fortune."

"Attend here," said Madame, and left the room. In her stead an assistant female arrived and began pulling out various half made up dresses from a concealed wardrobe in the wall.

"Do you think we have made a mistake coming here?" whispered Emily, startled at the dressmaker's lack of deference.

"No," said Clorinda. "I think we are absolutely in the right place. I feel that Madame Latour is a highly intelligent woman."

Barely had she finished speaking, when the French woman returned, carrying yet another pile of dresses over her arm. She cast a scornful look on the dresses laid out by her assistant and motioned them all away with a Gallic wave of her hand. Then she looked carefully at Clorinda, moving round her like a connoisseur admiring a statue. It would have been rude from anybody else, but from her this was obviously the concentrated assessment of an artist at work.

Picking out a pale green dress, and placing the others on the table, she held it against Clorinda's face. *"Non, ce n'est pas exacte.* It is better but it is not correct."

She did the same with an orange sarsanet, then with a yellow-green satin veiled with Brussels net. Both were rejected in silence. Turning back to the pile of gowns, she pulled out a clinging silk, also a pale green color but somehow subtly different. Its color seemed to play and shift.

"Eau de Nil," she said, ordering her assistant to hold it in place against Clorinda's face. Stepping

73

backward she gave another long look. "Yes, Mademoiselle," she said, in the tone of somebody who had finally come to a decision, "I can dress you."

"Thank you, Madame," said Clorinda simply. The two women looked at each other and something like an electric current of understanding seemed to run from the younger to the older. Both smiled.

"Perhaps we shall try this on more fully," suggested Madame Latour. "If Mademoiselle would be pleased to accompany me to the changing room, Madame can wait here for the transformation. There are many illustrations to employ the time of waiting," she added smiling slightly at Emily.

Feeling as if her fate hung in the balance, Clorinda followed her out of the room into a smaller chamber behind it. There with the help of innumerable pins and much twitching of its folds, the Eau de Nil dress was draped round her by the assistant. It was only half made up, Clorinda realized. "I have never heard of such a color," she confessed looking at Madame Latour for an explanation.

"It is so called after the waters of the Nile," was the reply. "There is a moment between day and night, when the sun hangs in the balance over the Nile. Then it is that the waters come alight with this color. Green fire is how some people describe it. Others say that it can be glimpsed elsewhere in the world, and call it the green flash of sunset.

"But nowhere but in Egypt can its full splendor be appreciated—except in this material. I have had it specially woven in Provence in France. If you look at it, you will see it is as if the waters were alight with phosphorescence."

Clorinda looked down at the gown she was

wearing. It was true. The effect was one of phosphorescence—the pale green color seemed to glow with yellow, orange and golden lights within it. As the material caught the light, or moved in its beams, these colors seemed to sparkle and flash within the delicately clinging silk. With a final adjustment of the material the French woman gestured for the assistant, kneeling on the floor with a handful of pins in her mouth, to get up.

"Madame in the next room will be needing refreshments," she ordered. Then as the woman hurried out, she led Clorinda in front of a full-length mirror. "It is my *chef d'oeuvre*, my masterpiece, that dress," she said. "I have waited to find somebody who might wear it."

What Clorinda saw in the mirror amazed her. It was a stranger, a stranger so beautiful as to almost take her breath away. The soft glinting folds of the material fell over her small breasts, and outlined their delicate immaturity. Her white shoulders rose from a dress that had been cut low for evening wear, but not so low as to be immodest.

Round her slender body the Eau de Nil colors glinted, shifted, changing and glowing; one moment revealing, the next concealing a form that might have belonged to the goddess Diana, virgin patroness of the moon. For the first time it was as if she was seeing herself, not as a child, but as a woman.

"Why, I am beautiful," she whispered. "Even the Duke will not be able to resist me now."

As the words escaped her, she could have bitten her tongue off. But it was too late. They had been spoken. Madame Latour's sensitive ears had picked them up.

"So, Mademoiselle, it is a question of a Duke, is it

75

then? And a matter of love? I have many women who tell me that they want to buy my so-excellent gowns. But when I am told that a woman must look beautiful, the most beautiful woman in London, then that is for a woman in love, I think?"

For a moment Clorinda was silent. What should she do? With a deep breath, she decided to throw herself upon the French woman's mercy. "It is not a question of love . . . not my love," she said slowly. "It is his love that I seek . . . I am the Duchess of Westhampton, you see."

At first the French woman's mobile face registered nothing, then an expression of enlightenment began to dawn. "So it is you who are the mystery Duchess," she said. "It is not how I thought. The town gossips are mistaken, I believe."

Clorinda blushed with embarrassment. "What do they say, these town gossips?" she queried bitterly.

"Are you sure that you would be happy, if I told you?" countered Madame Latour.

"I must know," said the girl baldly. "How else can I fight for my happiness?"

"They say," said Madame Latour with pity in her eyes, "they say that the Duke married in a fit of pique. That he chose a girl in the country of whom nobody had heard, and of whom he planned nobody should hear. They say that the duchess is a—how do you say?—a nobody, who will stay in the country and bear the little Dukes, and will not interfere with the *amour* of the Duke, his love."

"His love?" Clorinda's voice was low.

"That is what they *say*," parried the dressmaker. "Me, I do not go into society. I have chosen to make money for myself in a way that society does not approve, rather than live on charity.

"So it is as it is, but I hear what society is doing and saying—who more? It is to me that the rich ladies complain about their husbands. It is to me that they explain they must look beautiful—for this one or for this other. Me, I am discreet. I am just a dressmaker, so they tell me all."

She paused. "But you have not told me, Madame Duchess, why you came to me?" There was an odd note in her voice. Pity? Embarrassment? Clorinda was not sure.

"I have been told that you dress Lady Lancaster," said Clorinda abruptly. She wondered if she should have been so direct.

Madame Latour nodded knowingly. "Lady Lancaster wears my dresses and pays my bills—eventually. But she is an advertisement for my gowns. I will not deceive you, little one, about that woman. She has the beauty of an exotic orchid. One must acknowledge the truth. But is a beauty that is skin deep. I do not think that the Duke has a *veritable grand passion*. I think it is a *petit amour de plaisir*."

Without exactly comprehending everything, Clorinda nevertheless had her worst fears confirmed. The Duke, it seemed, had fallen in love with this Lady Lancaster. She sounded as if she was a sophisticated woman of the world. "Perhaps what I am doing is a mistake," she said. "I was not completely sure about this . . . this friend of my husband's.

"I . . . do not . . . entirely understand such things," she added painfully. "I know that the Duke does not love me, but I thought you could so dress me that he would not recognize his dowdy wife. Then

77

perhaps he might fall in love with me. I am sure he will never look twice at the countrified girl he married, but I hoped if I appeared in society incognito . . . but perhaps Lady Lancaster is too lovely?"

"She *is* lovely, but you will be lovelier still. That is a promise, *ma chère*," said the French woman. "One can only fight for love; one cannot promise victory. But will you trust me to make you a beauty? I must think for this night. It is not a scheme to be undertaken without thought."

"I will trust you," said Clorinda simply. Somehow she felt in capable and sympathetic hands. "Do you know the Duke?"

"I have met him . . . in circumstances which it is better that I do not tell you now," said Madame Latour evasively. Just then the assistant returned, bringing Emily with her.

"I could not wait," gasped her sister. "Oh Clorinda, you look wonderful. If only Mama could have seen you in that dress. She would have been so proud."

Madame Latour smiled. "Your schoolfriend, Mrs. Willoughby, must return tomorrow. The dress will be finished then, and I shall have searched our materials for a complete wardrobe. I think also, with your permission, I shall introduce her to a very old friend of mine, a Monsieur Lafayette who can aid her with some lessons in deportment."

"Is he a dancing teacher?" asked Emily innocently.

"He is very much not," said Madame Latour. "He is extremely well born, though a very old man and lives retired. I think he would very much like to meet this new young lady."

The name meant nothing to either Clorinda or Emily. "I will enjoy meeting him," said Clorinda politely.

The next day when she arrived at the Mayfair house of Madame Latour, she was led straight away into the back room.

There awaited her a huge pile of materials, clothes and accessories. It was like an Aladdin's cave. Clorinda had never before seen such a variety of materials and styles. There were simple muslins, silk, tulle, long lawn linens, satins veiled with Brussels net, sarsenets, and embroidered Indian muslins inserted with lace.

The proprietress greeted her affectionately with the warning words, "Now, Mademoiselle, since this is how you wish to be called, you must be prepared for the boredom. It is for us to work around you."

She spoke the truth. It seemed to Clorinda that she stood for hours being measured, tried, fitted— for day dresses, walking out dresses, pelisses, spencer jackets, redingotes, capes, traveling cloaks and, of course, ball gowns.

There were furs too—sable for trimming a pelisse, tiffets for walking out, and huge muffs instead of gloves. A glorious honey-colored full-length sable evening coat was the most exciting of all.

Gloves and bonnets and reticules to match the pelisses followed. There were spangled scarfs to be draped negligently round the shoulders, and soft Indian Cashmere shawls for warmth. A variety of ribbons, to be worn among the curls, were chosen with names like *amour de Venus* and *Pas ma faute*. There seemed no end to the number of clothes Clorinda would need. As piles were brought into the room, sorted through, tried, discarded or set aside for wear, Clorinda asked, "Do you usually outfit your customers so thoroughly?"

"You are not my usual customer," replied Madame Latour. "You have asked me to make you a new woman and this I shall do from top to toe. These things you could buy for yourself outside my establishment, but if you are to be beautiful then a guiding intelligence must be shed on even the smallest detail of what you wear." She brought forward a large pile of exquisitely embroidered handkerchiefs, then a pile of silk stockings.

"Will I really need six pairs?" asked Clorinda, somewhat aghast at such extravagance.

"To be beautiful you will need much of everything," said the French woman firmly. "It is expensive, no doubt," she added, "but if you aspire to the heights of the fashionable world, expense must not be spared. You cannot gain your heart's desire so cheaply, you know."

Her words caught Clorinda's curiosity. "If you will forgive me, Madame Latour," she said tentatively, "I should like to ask you how you became a couturier? It is surely not your natural metier?"

Madame Latour laughed. "You mean that I am a lady and not, as you expected, a tradeswoman?" she asked challengingly.

Clorinda flushed.

"Is that not true? Well, I will confess. I *am* a lady, more of a lady and of higher birth than many of those for whom I design dresses. My family, the Latours, were one of the oldest in Bordeaux. We could trace our ancestry back to Anne of Bordeaux," she said proudly.

"But how did you come to . . . ?" Clorinda

searched for the right way of posing her question. "How did you enter your profession?"

"It is an old story now. My family were ruined by the French revolution. My parents fell on the guillotine. I was eleven when the Terror broke out, and I was smuggled by some friends to England dressed as a gypsy child among a troop of Romanies.

"Most of my fellow sufferers returned after the Terror waned, but not I. My parents were dead, and by then I had fallen passionately, nay desperately in love, with an older man, an English aristocrat. We married—or at least I thought we had married but he had deceived me with a false ceremony. The details? They are as you might expect."

"What happened to the man?" said Clorinda urgently.

"When I discovered his deception I rooted my love for him out of my heart. I never saw him again. He died, I think, of an apoplexy. After his death his . . ." she paused, ". . . a relative found me and conveyed to me a considerable sum that he said he felt was mine by right. With it I was able to become a modiste. It is not an occupation that allows me to enter polite society, but the alternatives would have been a dreary existence as a governess, or perhaps companion to an old lady. Me, I value my independence."

"It cannot have been easy," said Clorinda.

"It was not . . . easy," said the French woman. "But I have been successful in my way. Because I pick and choose my customers, and because my dresses are original, I am able to charge outrageous prices. I can even be rude to my customers occasionally. They consider it proof of my exclusivity."

"They are beautiful dresses," said Clorinda looking down at a deceptively simply day dress in yellow ochre, with tinsel drawn work at the hem, and the same motif round the high goffered lawn ruff at the throat. "If clothes can give beauty, then I am sure these will."

"Beauty is in the heart, not just in the outward appearance," was the reply. "If you truly want to be beautiful, then you must be true to your heart. Yet a heart is a dangerous thing, as I know to my cost. It can deceive and ruin a woman, or indeed a man. Do you have a heart or are you lucky to feel nothing?"

"I do not know," Clorinda whispered. "If I feel anything, I think it is hatred, not love. I want the Duke to fall in love with me because he has ignored me and despised me and does not care for me. I want to teach him a lesson. I do not feel an atom of love for him." Her voice rose passionately.

"This is excellent," said Madame Genevieve. "Your heart is untouched. So much the better. You will be able to be gay and wilful and heartless. By keeping your own emotions cool, you will the better be able to charm him, entrap him and entice him. The arts of seduction can be learned."

"But who will teach me?" said Clorinda worriedly. "I do not have very much time to learn. And it seems as though I must rival no less a person than Lady Lancaster."

"I have your instructor," said Madame Latour, walking to a table on which lay a small silver bell. She rang it and the well-trained parlor maid arrived.

"Dobson, show in Monsieur Lafayette," she said.

She turned to the young girl and explained. "Monsieur Lafayette is a very old friend of mine. He is elderly now, but before the French Revolution he was perhaps the greatest leader of fashion in all France. The days of his gallantry ended when he lost the woman he loved.

"Then came the Revolution. He too escaped to England. Like me he prefers not to return to his native land. He lives retired today, almost a recluse. His title he has let slip into oblivion. But sometimes he vists me to talk over the old days. I have told him about you, and about your quest for love."

An erect old gentleman entered the room. He was dressed entirely in black, in the knee breeches and flared dress coat of an earlier and more formal age. His nose was acquiline and his face heavily lined. But his eyes were the fierce alert eyes of a hawk. His long slender fingers, white and smooth, denoted his aristocratic breeding. His whole bearing was proud and Clorinda at once recognized that this was a man whom no misfortunes could cow.

He crossed the room toward her, and with a formal bow took her hand and lifted it to his lips lightly. Clorinda blushed. "You are the young lady who wishes to captivate her husband," he said in an accented but charming voice. "I see beauty enough to captivate any man, though you are very young. Is your husband blind?"

"He is blind to me," said Clorinda. "But I am determined to open his eyes. He shall at least notice me."

"Bravo," said Monsieur Lafayette. "You have spirit, my infant. This is good. Now, if my dear friend Madame Latour will leave us, we will commence our first lesson. It is easier, I think, for just man and woman alone without an onlooker."

Clorinda was rather taken aback. What on earth did he mean by "lessons", and why should Madame

Latour leave the room. She looked enquiringly at the French woman, who merely said as she opened the door to go, "Have faith in Monsieur Lafayette, my dear. There is nothing he does not know about the art of gallantry."

"You may have faith, my infant," said the old man with a smile. "I am old enough to be your grandfather and I assure you that the things of passion are no longer of interest to me. I can, however, teach you a little about the way to behave."

Clorinda felt rather foolish. Of course, her fears had been ridiculous! She managed a rather shame-faced smile.

"We shall start with the curtsey," said Monsieur Lafayette. "You will curtsey to me, as if I am the Prince Regent."

Obediently Clorinda sank into a curtsey. She wondered what was the point of this.

"Now let us curtsey to a lover." By this time she decided he was slightly mad but she must humor him for the time being. Obediently she curtseyed a second time.

"No, no, no! That is the same curtsey, Mademoiselle. Unless I am to believe that you are imagining the Prince Regent as your lover. This will not do at all."

"What do you mean?" asked Clorinda a little impatiently. She did not understand what he was getting at.

"There are many curtseys, as many as there are distinctions between princes and men, and between men and women. There is the curtsey formal, of the kind you would make to the Prince. There is the curtsey antagonistic for the lady who is your rival.

84

There is the curtsey obedient, as for a husband. And there is, most important of all, the curtsey passionate for the man you love, or for the man who loves you whom you wish to encourage. So let us try this lover's curtsey again . . . slowly down . . . lower . . . lift your eyes and smile . . . that is better."

Obediently Clorinda had sunk to the floor, this time obeying his instructions about her eyes. "We shall practice the curtsey flirtatious with a fan," he then said, presenting her with beautifully carved little ivory fan which he took from his pocket. "Now you must look up . . . but not the full smile . . . a half smile with the fan a little in front of the mouth . . . the eyes looking over its top . . ."

The lesson continued. There were, it seemed, as many ways of holding out a hand to be kissed as there were curtseys. There was a distinction in the way a lace scarf might be draped round the shoulders—low conveyed a careless elegance, slightly higher a joyful enthusiasm.

Clorinda found herself practicing walking across the room—as if in a crowded salon, or in a formal ballroom, or in a ladies boudoir, or—such was Monsieur Lafayette's thoroughness—in a moonlit garden.

Slowly it became clear that he was teaching her nothing less than the art of love—the intuitive response to a situation that conveys encouragement, anger, pride or indifference by means of the smallest gesture. A flick of the fan, a lowering of the eyes, a half smile hovering about the lips—the slightest of these could convey a world of meaning.

"It is this you must learn," said the wise old gentleman. "Without this, a woman's beauty is like a statue's. It is cold and dead. It is the movement and the grace of that movement that brings the beauty to life."

By the time Clorinda had to return to her sister's, she felt that she had aged a thousand years in experience and subtlety. "Thank you, Monsieur Lafayette," she said. "You have given me something as valuable as Madame Latour's gowns."

"It has been a pleasure, my child," he said. "It is possible that my help to you may in some small part right a wrong that I did myself many years ago."

"What was that wrong?" Clorinda asked timidly.

"I shall tell you, my infant, when I am sure that you have captured the heart of your Duke," was all the elderly gentleman would say.

Back at her sister's house, Jack was waiting for her. "Clorinda," he said impetuously, as soon as she entered the room. "I have been waiting for you for hours." Then he stopped dead. His eyes widened in amazement.

"Good heavens, Clorinda," he said with an abrupt but brotherly lack of tact, "you look quite different. You look beautiful."

It was said with such genuine surprise that Clorinda could not help smiling. "That is praise indeed, coming from a brother," she said, giving him her hand to kiss and sinking to the floor in the most dignified of all the curtseys she had practiced. She could see that she had utterly astounded her scapegrace elder brother.

"Oh Lord, Clorinda," he said ruefully, "I dare say you may succeed with the Duke after all. Where did you learn these airs and graces?"

"With Monsieur Lafayette," said Clorinda.

"Never heard of him," said Jack quickly, "unless he's that French fellow who keeps the gambling hell in Clifford Street."

"He is nothing of the kind, let me tell you, Jack," said Clorinda ruffled. "He is a very aristocratic old gentleman who is teaching me how to get on. He has nothing to do with your sordid world of gambling hells."

"That's what I wanted to ask you, Clorinda," said her brother guiltily. "I don't know how it is but something seems to have got into the dice lately. Winterstoke tells me my luck must turn, but there are no signs. I am obliged to make a clean breast of it. I am in debt again, and worse than last time."

Clorinda looked at him sadly. She knew there was nothing fundamentally wrong with Jack, but it saddened her to know that he had got into a bad, deep drinking, hard playing set. Though he was only twenty-two, the marks of his dissipated nights were to be read on his face. "What I think you need, Jack, is something to do, so that you don't have to spend all your time going to the races and gambling."

"If only there was. What is a fellow to do? There's nothing I can do without money, except go to the devil."

"I shall ask the Duke, if ever my plan succeeds," said Clorinda. "He has been generous in the marriage settlements, and perhaps since he has paid off your debts once he will do so a second time. But I shall need your help, Jack."

"I have promised it already," he replied. "But I warn you I won't play the fool around you forever. Flesh and blood can't stand more than two weeks."

"Two weeks will be long enough for me to discover if my plan has any chance of working," said Clorinda optimistically. "Now you must tell me all you know about the Duke in London. How does he spend his time? Where is he to be found? Where can I meet him?"

"There's Jackson's sporting club but a lady could not exactly go there," said Jack cautiously. "You might meet him in Hyde Park driving those greys of his. Then in the evenings he usually looks in at a party or several. He'll be at Carlton House next week for the Prince Regent's ball, that's sure. Prinny wouldn't dare entertain without the Duke's attendance."

"What do you mean?" asked Clorinda.

"I mean that Prinny treats him as a sort of fashionable adviser. Needs the Duke's approval for his coats and for his horses, you know. And the Duke isn't half rude to him about them, sometimes.

"There's something you must do, Clorinda," Jack added suddenly. "If you are going to go to the Carlton House ball, and I must say I think you had better if you want to be sure of meeting the Duke— then you have got to learn to dance."

"I know the quadrille and the cotillion," said Clorinda. "But I am afraid I don't know how to waltz. That is to say, I have tried out the steps with Emily in the nursery, but I have not been taught it properly. And I have never danced it with a man."

At this moment Emily and Robert Willoughby walked into the room. "We shall teach you here and now," said Emily. "I shall play the piano and Robert shall dance with you. Jack can look on and tell us how you are doing from the outsider's point of view."

"That would be marvelous," said Clorinda clapping her hands with pleasure.

She knew that it was vital for her debut in society that she should waltz with grace. The dance was enormously popular. It had been introduced around 1807, and at first the leaders of society had said that it was "calculated to lead to the most licentious consequences."

But the dashing, the young and the fashionable had all taken to it, and no matter how much their elders complained, the ballrooms were full of couples merrily twirling around till giddy and flushed with exhaustion. "A coarse and vulgar romp" one writer called it, but the young people loved it.

Clorinda gingerly stepped into Robert's arms. She had never before been held so close to a man, save to her father. It seemed so odd. But Robert held her firmly in a brotherly embrace and she soon lost her shyness.

It was not till an hour later that Jack declared that her dancing would do. "She has got the idea now," he said, "but I think she still needs some practice at a proper ball. Your piano playing is not the same as an orchestra, Emily," he said.

Nobody could quarrel with that statement, least of all Emily. But the question was where could she practice?

"I know," said Emily suddenly. "What about Vauxhall Gardens? There's a masked ridotto tomorrow night. I saw a program."

"It's full of vulgar people," said Jack doubtfully.

"Yes, but we shall be masked," said Emily. "Besides, it's just what Clorinda needs—a place to practice without anybody knowing her."

For a moment it looked as if a long argument was going to break out between brother and sister, but Willoughby stepped into the breach. "If we go masked, Jack, there'll be no harm in it," he said. "Nobody will recognize any of us. It's an ideal place for Clorinda to practice with both of us."

"Thank you, Robert," said Clorinda. "It sounds so thrilling, please can we go? My first-ever ball! And I think the masks make it more romantic. Will the Duke be there?"

"The Duke of Westhampton?" said Jack sarcastically. "Not on your life, Clorinda. His Grace would never venture to set foot in such a vulgar place as Vauxhall Gardens."

(5)

His Grace the Duke of Westhampton *was* at Vauxhall Gardens.

Though he was masked, it was unmistakably him. The tall, arrogant figure seemed to tower above the other men, the strutting dandies, the portly aldermen, and young bucks. His black mask, through which Clorinda could see his eyes glitter, gave him a Demonic air.

His clothes alone betrayed him. Unlike the dandies who were conspicious by their garments, the Duke was dressed with impeccable discretion and perfect taste. But the tightly fitting stockinet pantaloons, and the coat so beautifully tailored that at least two men must have helped him to shrug it on, betrayed the tailoring of a master.

Hessian boots, shining with champagne and blacking, and cut with tassels completed his ensemble. Nothing particularly caught the eyes, except that every garment was exquisitely made.

And the careless limbs, powerful thighs and strong shoulders would have made him remarkable in any company. The way he stood, the way he walked, his every movement conveyed the strength of a man who was perfectly fit.

At his waistcoat, which was discreetly but richly embroidered, hung a quizzing glass that the Duke was using to survey the scene in front of him. He looked bored.

But it was not just the man who caught Clorinda's eye. It was the woman with him.

She too was dark, with locks as black as a raven's plumage. She had dressed with unbelievable daring. Her startling red gown, the color of blood, was cut so low that it revealed almost all the creamy swell of her bosom. Round her neck, falling over her breasts, there flashed a circlet of rubies. She wore a crimson mask.

She was talking in an animated way to the Duke. From the sight of her gestures, Clorinda gathered that she was teasing him, daring him, provoking him. Once she threw back her heavy black locks and laughed aloud, exposing her glorious bosom in a way which Clorinda knew was improper, but had to admit was incredibly provocative.

The two of them, both masked, both magnificent in their mindless disregard of the crowd, seemed the perfection of elegance. The dark Duke, a cynical smile playing round his lips, and the sophisticated woman glancing up through dark lashes to meet his gaze might have been out of some exotic tale of Arabian nights.

As Clorinda watched, she saw the woman give the Duke a long, lingering smoldering look of such naked hunger that Clorinda was almost embarrassed. The Duke returned the gaze, still smiling cynically, but with a darkening in his eyes which showed that he too was experiencing a response to that hunger.

The exchange of glances made Clorinda shiver. Was this the love of which she was ignorant? Was this naked hunger love? It was a cruel emotion, it seemed to her—a feeling powerful but somehow frightening.

She felt pathetically young and ignorant.

At first the evening to Vauxhall Gardens had been delightful. The party of four, all masked, Emily, Robert, Jack and Clorinda had arrived by boat, hiring a six oar barge at Westminster which took them across the river to the Gardens. The gentle plopping of the oars, broken by the occasional mutter from the oarsmen, the tranquil Thames, and the sight of the pleasure gardens just as dusk began to fall, was an enchantment in itself.

Vauxhall Gardens, itself, was the scene of a glittering throng—or so it seemed to country-bred Clorinda. "There are so many people," she confided to Jack.

"I'd say London was thin of company," said her down-to-earth brother, casting a knowing eye at the people around them. "It's cits and tradesmen mostly."

But even he allowed that the gardens, themselves, were beautiful. Among the trees, thousands of lamps glimmered and winked in the gathering twilight, their different hues mingling with the brightly colored dresses of the women to make a kind of jeweled exoticness.

In the wonderful Eau de Nil dress, with its soft folds gathered high under her small pointed breasts, Clorinda was attracting no little attention. But she was unconscious of the admiring glances and hopeful looks cast at her. She and Emily made a striking pair. Both girls were innocent of all jewelry. Instead they had simple ribbons in their hair. Emily's divinely fair locks clustered round her head, and with a pale blue gown that matched her gentle eyes, she looked like a princess in one of those fairy tales.

Beside her, her sister had a most outstanding, almost eerie, charm. She had tied a white ribbon among her curling red tendrils. In the lamplight her skin glowed like ivory, catching the colors from the lamps and throwing it back to the observer. The green of her dress and the green of her eyes through the mask were unusual enough to capture the interest of the most experienced connoisseur of female beauty.

It was Robert Willoughby who voiced what all must think. "Nobody in the Gardens can rival you two sisters," he said. He smiled to see that Clorinda was blushing at even so simple a compliment. With the faint touch of pink in her cheeks, she looked almost ethereal in her beauty.

It had been a wonderful start to the evening, Clorinda thought, as she strolled round the Rotunda with her sister and the two men. Now everything was spoiled by the appearance of the Duke. Instead of being able to enjoy herself simply and peacefully, her heart was a raging inferno of emotion.

She wondered if she should tell the others. But, realizing that it might spoil their pleasure, she decided not. After all their masks should prove protection enough.

"He has not seen me," she said to herself. But even as she tried to still her fear, a wave of panic swept over her. For a moment she thought she might faint. Her whole being cried out. Only a superhuman effort of will kept her upright.

Somehow she would have to fight this panic. If she was to meet the Duke again—and this was the central point of her plan—then she must overcome her fear. Emily was saying something to her, a remark on the beauty of the surroundings. Clorinda managed a tremulous smile in response.

Her sister looked anxiously at her, "What is wrong, Clorinda dear?" she asked softly so that the two men would not hear.

"There is nothing wrong . . . nothing. It is just that there are so many people. . . . have never before . . . been in such a crowd."

Robert Willoughby led the party to one of the pavilions where supper was served, and as they went Clorinda noticed that the flamboyant pair had somehow merged into the moving shifting throng. Her presence of mind returned to her, and she was able to make amusing conversation with her companions.

Willoughby had arranged the evening in style. At a well-sited table they could watch the entertainment of the passing crowd. He ordered the special punch for which Vauxhall was famous and the traditional dish of ham. The ham was celebrated, not only for its delicate flavor, but for the thinness of its slices. It was said that a carver could divide one ham thin enough to pave the whole garden with its slices.

Lemonade for the ladies and a selection of tarts and custards and cheesecakes to follow finished a repast that Jack voted "fit for the Prince Regent, himself." And indeed the Prince had visited Vauxhall Gardens only recently. Even Clorinda managed to sample a slice of ham and nibble at a cheesecake.

After the dishes had been cleared Robert placed his hand on her shoulder in brotherly fashion and suggested, "Perhaps we should take a stroll around the groves. They are very pretty now that the dark has come and the lamps are all out."

"Yes, indeed," said Clorinda with spirit. "I am enjoying myself so much. I hope also, Robert, that you will gratify me with a dance later on. It is for this we came, after all. I must practice my steps." She gave a little laugh of pleasure. Her fears had vanished. The Duke was nowhere to be seen. Now she could relax and enjoy herself.

It was truly a fairytale evening. Strolling through the statues, the trees and the crowds, there were many sights to admire and to be interested by. Though dark had fallen, it was a balmy evening just freshened by a slight breeze which lifted the red-gold tendrils of her hair and made them play round her heart-shaped face.

Strolling down a main alleyway, Clorinda suddenly realized something was wrong. She had left her reticule behind at their table. "Wait for me, Jack," she cried impetuously. "I must find my reticule." Before either man could volunteer their aid, she had turned on her heels and sped back toward the pavilion where they had been dining.

"She's as much of a romp as ever," grumbled Jack. "I'd have fetched it for her, if she'd only have waited." But the slim figure had disappeared through the crowds.

Clorinda weaved her way through the passing couples back to their table. To her relief she saw the elegant little bag, matching her dress, sitting safely on the chair where she must have left it. Irresistably she could not help taking a swift glance round to see if the tall figure of the Duke was anywhere nearby. It was not. "Now I can enjoy the evening," she thought, "He must have left."

She turned back toward the alleyway where she thought she had left the other three. Pushing her way eagerly past the people, she was half way down before she realized she must have come in the wrong direction. There was no sign of Emily or Jack or Robert.

Looking round rather wildly she started to retrace her steps. Perhaps they had turned off through the trees. She turned down one of the smallers walks. At the end, she thought she saw three figures that were them. Running gaily towards them she cried, "Wait for me."

One of the two men turned round. It was a complete stranger, and from the look of him, not even a gentleman. "Why, my dear," he said in an odiously familiar tone, "of course we'll wait."

"I'm sorry," gasped Clorinda. "I thought you were somebody else." Again she turned back, taking no notice of the vulgar cry behind her of "Will not I do in his place, sweetheart?"

Her heart was beating rapidly, and she was now seriously confused. The colored lamps which had looked so pretty only a few minutes before, were now misleading. She could not see properly by their light to know who was passing. Running back down the walk, she found herself at the junction of the ways that she did not recognize at all.

A large party of young men was advancing from one end. They had linked arms, and were obviously in a boisterous mood. Halloos and shouts were coming from them. Desperately Clorinda glanced round for help. There was nothing for it, she must turn into one of the even smaller dark walks.

As she rounded the corner, she cannoned straight into a gentleman. To her relief she noticed that he was soberly, if expensively, dressed and obviously older than the young blades she had avoided.

"Oh Sir," she gasped. "I am lost. Can you help me?"

With a studiedly elegant bow, he replied, "I am entirely at your service, my beauty. So much charm must surely need attendance."

His tone, though polite, was nevertheless silky with insolence. Looking closer, Clorinda realized that she had not been mistaken in thinking him older, but there was nothing fatherly about his eyes, as they raked down her form.

"Thank you, Sir," she replied stiffly. "I would be grateful if you might escort me back to the main alleyway. I am with a party of friends, but have unfortunately lost my way."

He held out his arm with something of a flourish. Clorinda had misgivings about accepting his help, but just as she was about to draw back she heard the whoops and noises from the party of drunken blades coming toward them. Rather than face them, she placed her hand gingerly upon his arm.

Sedately he led her down the dark walk. "Are you sure this is the right direction?" she asked. The alley appeared to get darker, and it seemed as if the colored lamps were more sparsely furnished with every step.

"Venus, you are in good hands," he said. "I am

Lord Winterstoke." Through the slits of his dark blue mask she could see his eyes glistening.

She recognized the name. It was none other than Jack's mentor, whose influence on the young boy seemed so disastrous. For a second she considered telling him who she was, then further reflection decided that this would be folly. Her impetuous actions had led her to this pass.

"Thank you, Lord Winterstoke," she said coolly. "I am grateful for your escort. But I believe that we are not proceeding toward the center of the Gardens. I see I must shift for myself."

She would have taken her arm away from his, only at this moment he pulled her closer toward him. "You are here with your lover, perhaps," he said thickly. She wondered if he was drunk. "Let the foolish dog go hang. Come with me, my pretty."

"I am with a party, Sir." Clorinda looked round desperately. In the darkness, broken only by the very occasional lamp dimly burning, she could see nobody. "I must return," she pleaded.

His hand was now gripping her arm tightly, so tightly that it hurt. He had halted altogether, and put himself in front of her so that he barred her progress. She could feel his fingers digging into her flesh. "Let me go, Sir," she cried. "If you are a gentleman at all, you will let me go."

"You are too pretty to escape," he said, holding her at arms' length in a way that gave him the chance to look her up and down at his leisure. His very glance seemed to make the blood rise in her cheeks.

She gave a little cry of fear. It only served to inflame him. Still grasping her arm, he swung round as if to embrace her. Pulling against him with all her

99

might, Clorinda realized that he was as strong as a much younger man. In anguish, she slapped him hard on the face. The blow rang out in the alleyway, and left a red mark on his cheek.

He only laughed. "I like a woman of spirit," he said in a voice that made her blood run cold. "Opposition lends enchantment to the act. I shall tame you, wild filly that you are."

She knew she could not escape him. Inch by inch he pulled her close to him. His thin mouth was twisted into a gloating smile. His eyes were glittering through the mask. To her mounting horror she noticed that his tongue passed over those thin lips leaving a wet mark behind it.

Mad with fear she tried one last appeal. "Lord Winterstoke, I implore you . . ." was all she could manage. She felt his hot breath on her face and his features swam before her eyes. The hot and greedy mouth closed brutally over hers, so fiercely that it seemed to bruise her flesh.

She felt his hands on her body, exploring, invading, desecrating it through the thin silk of her dress. He had his fingers twisted in her hair so that she could not move. Blindly she tried to move her lips from his, but with a wrench he pulled them back again.

Just as she thought she could bear it no more, the lustful face swung out of her vision. Instead of the cruel hot hands she felt a cool fingertip touch on her arm. "Lord Winterstoke was bothering you, I believe," came a cold and formal voice.

"I was so frightened . . ." was all that Clorinda could gasp. The world seemed to swim around her —the dim lamps, the dark alleyways, the erect figure of the man standing in the shadows beside her. "Do not leave me," she pleaded.

For a second she clutched at the newcomer's arm to steady herself. Then the feeling of faintness passed, and she began to think again. At all costs she must avoid a vulgar scene.

Lord Winterstoke had been sprawled on the grass in front of her. The stranger must have knocked him down. He began to get up, brushing his coat where it had mud upon it. The scowl on his face showed the depths of his resentment. Clorinda could feel the unspoken antagonism between the two men. She must smooth this moment over, at whatever cost, and prevent them from flying at each other's throats.

She took her hand from the newcomer's arm. Something was familiar about him but in the shock of the moment she could not think what. In the darkness of the alleyway she could see very little, except his tall, towering figure.

"Lord Winterstoke had offered to escort me back to my party." She lied smoothly, but there was an undertone of terror still in her voice. "He may have lost his way . . . I believe . . . I should be grateful if you can aid me."

"I know very well what Lord Winterstoke was doing," said her rescuer curtly. "I am well acquainted with My Lord Winterstoke's activities. I shall see you safely back to your party, but I am sure that Lord Winterstoke would wish to offer his apologies to you for this unfortunate occurrence." There was a ring of steel in his voice that made it clear that he intended to be obeyed.

It was the Duke. In a flash Clorinda realized.

The tall figure, the voice, that somewhat bored drawl. It could be no other.

She turned from the handsome figure by her side to contemplate the elderly man in front of her. As her self possession returned she could see that he was considerably older than the Duke. His face was lined, and somehow marked as if evil had left its stamp on it. The thin lips still curved brutally. She shuddered a little.

"I should be delighted to apologize for my *unlucky* encounter with you, Duke," said Lord Winterstoke silkily. "May I know the name of the lady whom I may have inadvertently distressed?" He did not sound in the least sorry. Indeed he seemed to gloat over the reminder that he had forced her in his arms.

Clorinda put up her chin. "I accept your apology, Lord Winterstoke," she said firmly. "My name can be of no interest to you." She sensed that he was about to kiss her hand. Remembering Monsieur Lafayette's lesson, she sank into a very low, very dignified, and utterly formal curtsey.

Nonplussed the old rake turned away. Then placing her hand on the Duke's arm, she remarked in a voice that she hoped bore no signs of trembling, "Who is Lord Winterstoke?"

"He is very rich, very old and most unsuitable as an escort for any young girl," said the Duke shortly. "I can only advise you to keep out of his way. It is quite wrong for any female to have dealings with him at all."

"I was here with some friends," Clorinda found herself apologizing. "I left my reticule at the table and ran back for it. Then I could not find my party.

I was lost. Then I met him and he offered to help me find them."

"It was extremely foolish of you to have anything to do with him," said the Duke in blighting tones.

They were walking up the small dark alleyway, toward the more lighted part. For a second he halted. Rudely he said to her, as they stopped near one of the more strongly glowing lights, "You smell of rosewater. How old are you?"

Clorinda had the oddest sensation that he was thinking of kissing her. But it could not have been true. He made no move.

"How old are you?" he repeated.

"I cannot think it is any of your business," she said crossly. "I am seventeen."

"Too young to be allowed to roam in Vauxhall Gardens by yourself. I wonder that your friends did not take better care of you," was the reply. His words were cold.

Clorinda had never hated him more, but she knew that politeness required she should thank him. "I am grateful for your intervention," she said stiffly. "I shall do my best to remember that you have offered me advice in what I hope is a kindly spirit. But I do not think you have any right to lecture me."

"My dear girl, I have every right. What is to stop me from treating you as Winterstoke did? Come, come. If I lecture you, you should be thankful I am not a Winterstoke. Take my lectures with a good grace, and recollect that you are lucky I am a gentleman."

"I think you are being amazingly impertinent," said Clorinda. "Now we are back in one of the main alleyways, I need trouble you for your escort no longer. I can now return to my table. I should think my friends will have returned by now."

"I shall escort you, you foolish girl," said the Duke firmly. "You have no more sense than a kitten. Like it or not, you need my protection."

Seething with anger, Clorinda took refuge in silence. There was much justice in what he said, she acknowledged. But she could not understand why he was so rude in every way. It was as if he made no effort to display even the normal courtesies.

She stole a glance at him to see how he was taking her silence. The Duke's face wore its normal bored and impassive look. She could not tell from it what was passing through his mind. This man beside her was so off-hand, so utterly impervious to other people's feelings, that she longed to humble his overweening arrogance.

He broke the silence once. "Who are you?" he said. "And who are these friends who so signally have failed to chaperone you?"

"I shall not tell you," said Clorinda with spirit. It did not seem to her that now was the moment to reveal even her pretended identity. More than ever she was thankful for the mask.

"I shall find out," taunted the Duke.

"You must do as you please," she retorted. She wondered whether he would recognize her brother Jack and sister Emily behind their masks. Probably not. He had met Emily only once, and Jack only occasionally. There was no reason why he should associate them with the unknown young woman he had rescued fainting in Lord Winterstoke's evil embrace.

As they walked towards the pavilion, Clorinda

saw with satisfaction that Emily, Robert and Jack were there looking anxiously round for her. As she stepped up, her hand on the Duke's arm, she almost laughed—their expressions were so dumbfounded.

"Emily," she said, entering into the spirit of the thing. "This gentleman has kindly helped me find my way back to the table. I was lost in the alleyway. He and I have retained our incognito, but I am sure you would want to thank him."

Emily blushed. "We were so worried." Turning to the Duke, she held out her hand. "Thank you for looking after her. I fear there are some rather rough people about."

"You should warn your friend to behave with greater circumspection," said the Duke coldly. Then to Clorinda's surprise he added, "She is under your chaperonage, I presume. It is easy for you to show your thanks to me. I should like to dance with the lady whom I have rescued."

Emily looked slightly anxious. She had obviously failed to recognize the Duke. "How odd," thought Clorinda, "I should have thought anybody would know him instantly."

She felt elated. "Emily, please let me. This gentleman has been so kind."

"You will bring her back very soon, will you not?" said Emily to the Duke.

"Madam, if you are anxious about my intentions," he said dryly, "you may take yourself to the Rotunda and watch us on the floor."

With that, he offered Clorinda his arm and she walked off with him toward the orchestra. She felt deliriously happy. The evening, the crowds and the excitement had gone to her head like wine. The narrowness of her escape from the rakish Lord Winterstoke was forgotten in this sudden access of high spirits. It was as if she was floating on air.

"It will be the first time I have danced the waltz in public," she confided to the Duke, "so you will have to forgive me if I tread on your toes."

His aquiline face softened. "It will be a privilege to be the first man to waltz with you," he said. "This must be your debut in London. I am sure that in a few days' time I shall have to queue up to take my turn with many other eager partners."

He put his hand round her waist and swept her onto the floor. At first Clorinda could only worry about her steps. She concentrated on getting them right. Then she became aware of the nearness of him. Very seriously and very simply she lifted her eyes to his face as they twirled around the floor.

"Why are you so abrupt with me?" she asked him. "I do not think I deserved that scolding you gave me after you had rescued me from Lord Winterstoke. It was not very gallant of you."

He was silent for a moment. Then with the suspicion of a smile he looked down at her and said equally seriously, "I think you need the protection of somebody. You are very young, you know. You must learn that there are men who, though their rank is that of gentlemen, do not behave as they should. In particular at a masked ball there are always some vulgar scenes. I think this must be your first visit to London."

"It is not my first visit," replied Clorinda thinking of that nightmare day when this very man had made her his wife. "But this is my first happy visit. My only other expedition to London was more of a business transaction."

"I see you are teasing me," said the Duke. "You

are too young to be engaged in business activities."

Clorinda did not dare explain. It was dangerous ground. Just then the music increased into a crescendo, and she felt almost breathless with it. When she had practiced her steps with Robert, it had not been like this.

Now she was in the arms of a skilful dancer, she felt she was a bird soaring above the clouds. Every movement he made was perfectly in time, and her body responded to him as if they had known each other for a lifetime. She wondered if anything could possibly compare with this, whether ever again she would experience this haunting sense of utter harmony and rhythmical pleasure.

"I am so happy," she could not help saying.

"I am glad you are enjoying yourself." The Duke spoke coldly, even formally, as if he disapproved of her exhibiting her emotions too freely. Then, as if to dash her mood of elation, he added, "I really do not think you should be at a masked ridotto at all. It is not the thing."

"You really do say unpleasant things," said Clorinda indignantly.

She thought she saw a look of surprise flicker in the Duke's eyes. Obviously few people talked to him like that. "Bravo, I see you are a girl of spirit," was all that he said.

"Are you trying to flirt with me?" said Clorinda daringly.

"Not in the least," he replied. "Is that what you would like me to do? I am always happy to oblige ladies with flirtations, though I confess I had not thought you would enjoy them after your experiences earlier this evening."

The rebuke made her blush. She felt she had

got the worst of the exchange. Seeing her flush, the Duke added more kindly, "You know you are much too young and innocent to start up a flirtation—unless I am much mistaken, I only flirt with ladies who know the rules of the game, and it is a dangerous game as well as a pleasant one."

The music ended. There seemed nothing else to say. With heightened color Clorinda returned to her sister on the Duke's arm. She found her pleasure in that wonderful moment of dancing marred by the sparring conversation they had had.

With a formal acknowledgement of her head, she thanked her partner for the dance.

"It was my pleasure," he replied equally formally. Then turning to Emily he added, "I think a closer chaperonage would be to her advantage."

"How unhandsome of you! I thought you were going to keep my secret!" Clorinda was outraged. "This is treachery," she said angrily.

"Not treachery, merely common sense. I found your friend all but fainting in the drunken embraces of Lord Winterstoke in a dark alleyway. I do not know what might have happened but for my timely arrival," he explained to Emily.

Then turning to Clorinda he added, "If I believed you were capable of dealing with such as Winterstoke I would keep your so-called secret. But after talking to you I know that you are far too unworldly to know how to look after yourself."

Emily looked confused and angry. Jack too was evidently outraged, but Clorinda noticed with approval that he kept his tongue silent. It was Robert who found the words for them all. "We are truly grateful for your intervention," he said quietly. "I know a little of Lord Winterstoke and what I know I do not like. I would very much like to call upon you tomorrow and express my gratitude, if you would be so kind as to drop your incognito."

"No, do not let us do that," cried Clorinda hastily. "I am sure it is far more romantic to remain strangers to each other. Besides there is no reason why we should meet again."

For a moment it seemed as if the Duke was going to say something, but suddenly all five of them became aware that a sixth person had joined them. In a wave of heady perfume, the exotic dark-haired woman that Clorinda had seen earlier with the Duke came over to their table.

With a total disregard for all of them except the Duke, the magnificent woman spoke to him. "Julian, I am utterly and totally consumed with boredom and beg that you will rescue me immediately," she said imperiously. "It is a positive hurly burly of cits and other vulgar persons tonight. I swear Vauxhall Gardens is as tedious as it ever was."

With a glance toward Robert and Jack, she nodded casually, but took no notice of Emily or Clorinda. The Duke looked at her for a moment as if calculating her mood then said, "If it grows tedious then perhaps we should leave."

Bowing towards Emily and Clorinda, he added, "Goodbye, my unknown fair ladies. I trust you require my services no longer?"

"Thank you so much," said Emily softly. Clorinda said nothing. She did not feel like thanking him particularly.

As he and the woman turned to go, Clorinda heard her remark in perfectly audible tones: "Julian, where did you pick up such extraordinarily dull people? I swear you have a taste for the bourgeoisie."

"We are not extraordinary people," said Clorinda crossly to her sister. "Nor are we bourgeois. I think it is her who is vulgar. Did you ever see such a low cut dress?"

"I swear they are both familiar," said Jack. "I'll lay odds I've seen her somewhere—and he too. He is obviously a man of ton." Then changing his tone, he said, "What's this farrago of nonsense about Winterstoke, then, Clorinda? You have got yourself into a scrape again, I see. You are incorrigible."

"It's not nonsense at all. Your precious friend Lord Winterstoke . . . tried to kiss me." Clorinda's voice was small and tight with the shame. "I think he was drunk."

"Well, heaven knows there are plenty of *filles de joie* and Cyprians around tonight," said Jack, uncomfortable at his sister's reply. "With that mask on, and with no more sense than a butterfly, Winterstoke must have thought you were one of them."

"One of what?" asked Clorinda innocently. Her brother did not reply.

Dancing with Jack and then with Robert was fun, Clorinda had to admit. The evening was still warm, and the lamps were as beautiful as ever. But somehow the romance and excitement had gone out of the occasion with the Duke's departure.

It was not that he was a romantic figure, she decided. Far from it. He had behaved in an odiously old-fashioned way, lecturing her about her behavior and the need for her to be more closely chaperoned.

"Yet you can't ignore him," thought Clorinda as

she twirled round the dance floor in her brother's firm arms. "He is sometimes quite hateful, but he is not dull. Nor is he like that horrid Lord Winterstoke." She thought of the drunken rake's hot breath and brutal pressure on her lips and could not help trembling.

"I hope I shall not have to meet Lord Winterstoke again," she said to Emily, as the barge conveyed the tired party back to the Westminster steps."

"I hope so too," said Emily softly so that Jack should not hear. "I have heard some horrid stories about him. They say he has ruined some woman and is utterly without scruples."

That night she came to Clorinda's bedchamber to kiss her goodnight. In her white cotton nightgown her young sister looked ridiculously childish. "I want to tell you something. You must not tell Jack," said Clorinda. "The man who rescued me . . . from Lord Winterstoke . . . was the Duke of Westhampton. Do you think he . . . liked me?"

"I don't know," said Emily in astonishment. "Are you sure, Clorinda? Oh, I do hope this all works out all right. I think the Duke might be very angry when he discovers the trick we have been playing on him."

"Who do you think that lady with him was?" came her sister's small but persistent voice.

"I cannot imagine. It is late, Clorinda. You should be asleep." Emily's voice was unconvincing.

"I think it was Lady Lancaster," said Clorinda in a small voice.

"I am sure it makes no odds who it was," said Emily with an attempt at briskness. "Perhaps it was not the Duke at all, Clorinda. I did not recognize him, neither did Jack. You may have imagined it."

"Well, I didn't," said her sister firmly. "I know it

was the Duke, and I think he behaved in a very boring way."

As her sister kissed her lovingly and left the room, Clorinda's words seemed to echo in the silent night. Snuggled down into the blankets, the little red curly head could not be rid of the thought that her last remark was a lie. Even the thought of the Duke seemed to cast all her emotions—fear, hatred, liking —into a turmoil.

"He is . . . not . . . boring," said Clorinda aloud to her pillow.

(6)

"It is time," Clorinda announced to Emily the following morning, "that I met the Duke and began my campaign to fascinate him. But how am I going to start?"

"I think we shall have to go to Hyde Park," said Emily. "The Duke is well known for his wonderful horses, and he can usually be found driving his grays in his phaeton. He had it specially designed for him."

"We must get Jack to take us both," said Clorinda firmly. "I am sure that an early morning stroll will be good for him."

The two girls were sitting in the breakfast room of the small but elegant London house of Robert Willoughby. The more sophisticated stars in the London scene might languish in bed sipping their chocolate before rising, but both Clorinda and Emily had been brought up in the country way of rising early. Besides, both agreed that it had been an agreeable evening but not exhausting.

The girls might be up early, but their brother Jack was most certainly not. It was therefore late in the morning by the time he responded to the message delivered to his lodgings. "Heavens, girl," he said to Clorinda as the butler showed him in eventually, "a man must tie his cravat, you know. Mine takes at least half an hour, and I don't think it has ever taken me less than an hour to dress in town."

"It is good for you to get up early," said his younger sister firmly. "If I can, after last night's dancing, why cannot you?"

"It is not just dancing," admitted Jack. "I had to drop in at the Club last night, then I had a bet on the number of times Black Bess would stumble over the course at Newmarket. A man must pay his debts, you know. I was expected."

"Well, I'm very surprised," cried Clorinda. "I didn't think you ever paid your debts, Jack."

"This was a debt of honor. They're different. I wouldn't go throwing my money away paying a lot of tradesmen." explained Jack. "Anyway," he added, "now you've dragged me here I see that you are not dressed for walking yourself. I shall have a glass of madeira while you put on your pelisse."

Clorinda was about to say something angrily about late-risers when she decided a scowling Jack would hardly lend grace to their proposed expedition to the park. Leaving Emily to order the madeira, she ran upstairs to put on her new soft leather half boots, and new pelisse. With its dark green folds around her, trimmed with swansdown at the hem, and a coquettish bonnet with the same trimming placed over her red-gold curls, she pirouetted in front of the mirror.

"Madame Genevieve is a genius," she thought to herself. The reflection that met her eye was perfect from the top of the frivolous, almost absurd, little bonnet to the neat little boots underneath. Picking up an equally frivolous, and shockingly expensive, parasol, she was ready for Hyde Park.

With a beautiful sister on either arm, Jack proceeded to the park, grumbling in the unappreciative tones of a brother. It was a glorious day. White fluffy clouds chased over a peerless blue sky, driven by a breeze just strong enough to riffle the swansdown on Clorinda's bonnet, and bring a becoming glow to her cheeks.

No sooner had they entered the Park gates than Clorinda realized that Emily had been absolutely right. All the fashionable world seemed to be there. There were groups of gentlemen, escorting ladies, strolling down the grassy turf, admiring the flowers, or on the lookout for friends like the three de Villiers. Others had chosen to ride showy horses up and down Rotten Row—sometimes unaccompanied, sometimes in groups of two or three ladies and the equivalent number of gentlemen.

Every kind of vehicle and equipage seemed to crowd the roads. The more sedate parties traveled in highly polished barouches or landaus, open carriages that allowed the occupants to stop frequently to exchange greetings or gossip with friends. But most noticeable was the endless variety of phaetons, slightly built four-wheeled driving vehicles that could be styled either relatively sedately, or sprung high so that the driver's seat was slung over the wheels in what seemed a most dangerous fashion.

These equipages were usually completed by the addition of a groom, who could leap off the vehicle and hold the restless horses, if the driver wished to stop for a talk. In the same way, lifts could be given and received, by the simple method of leaving the groom behind—to be picked up once a turn round the park had been completed.

There was one phaeton Clorinda could not help noticing. It was built with a particularly high perched seat that swayed dangerously at the corners, and it seemed to be proceeding at a pace more than uncommonly fast. "Who is that?" she asked Jack.

"Lord, how like a girl not to recognize those horses," said her brother scornfully. "I thought you said you'd been overtaken by them on the London road. They're the Duke's grays, of course, and that's the Duke driving them. The very man we want. I must say, Clorinda," he added with boyish enthusiasm, "he may be a very poor husband, but he's a tremendously good driver. Look at those devilishly light hands! And see how he takes those corners!"

Just then the dashing vehicle swerved round and came straight toward them. The pace was reckless. As they came closer, Clorinda could recognize the grays. What other pair would go so fast in such a crowded avenue?

Just as she thought they would all three be run down by the noble beasts, the carriage halted. The groom jumped from his seat and ran round to hold the sweating, stamping horses whose foaming bits showed their desire to continue at that breakneck speed.

The Duke leaned down from his uncertain and perilous perch seat. "Good morning, Villiers," he said. "I hope you are going to introduce me to your fair companions."

Then, as if he noticed and recognized Emily for the first time, he said, "Forgive me, Mrs. Willoughby. I was so busy with the reins I did not immediately perceive that it was you. We have only met briefly, but I hope it gives me the right to wish you good fortune in your newly married life."

"Thank you, Your Grace," said Emily blushing slightly. "May I take the opportunity to present one of my dearest friends, Miss de Vere, who is staying with us for a while. She has been admiring your grays, as have we all."

"They are magnificent animals," acknowledged Clorinda with a winning smile. She did not entirely feel like smiling, since she was in a flurry of nervousness wondering if the Duke recognized her as the same young woman he had waltzed with the night before. The very thought that he had found her struggling to evade Lord Winterstoke made her want to blush. But she knew that she must act, to begin with at least, as if they were strangers to each other.

The Duke was dressed, as ever, in his inimitable style. Beside his snowy white and deceptively simple cravat, Jack's elaborate neck adornment looked faintly absurd. Yet Clorinda knew that the Duke's apparently simple style was the result, no doubt, of hours of effort.

"If you admire my horses, Miss de Vere, may I invite you to sample their paces? I would be honored and flattered if you would allow me to drive you for a turn around the park," said the Duke smoothly.

His elaborate compliment slightly irritated Clorinda. "I do not know if it would be suitable to drive with you, Your Grace," she said, primly.

"It is quite suitable," said Emily quickly. "Look around and you will see that it is quite the fashion for gentlemen to drive ladies for a short while."

Clorinda climbed up onto the perch seat beside the Duke. It seemed a very long way up and extremely hazardous. "I would help you up," apologized the man beside her, "but I have my hands full with my pair."

It was no less than the truth. The horses were restlessly fidgeting and anxious to go. When the groom stood away from them, they leaped forward with a terrifying jerk. For a moment Clorinda waited until the Duke had them firmly under control.

She had decided to reveal to the Duke who she was—well, not that she was his wife, Clorinda de Villiers, rather that she had been the unknown stranger whom he had aided the night before at Vauxhall Gardens. "You were the gentleman who came to my rescue last night," she said in her musical voice. "I owe you my thanks."

"Did you think I had not recognized you?" said the Duke impatiently. "You have no need to tell me. Just one glimpse at those red locks, and I knew it must be you. I told you I should find out who you were."

Clorinda wanted to smile at this last remark. He was so confident. He might have recognized her in the Park, but he still had no idea that the woman he was talking to was the dowdy wife he thought was still in the country!

"I have a very good eye for beauty," went on the Duke. "My friends tell me that I have unerring taste in women's charms."

"I don't think this is the kind of conversation we should be having," said Clorinda with spirit. "Last night you scolded me for being careless about chaperones, and now you are paying me compliments when I am all alone in your phaeton without any chaperone at all. If I remember your rebukes correctly last night, you were almost suggesting that I should go nowhere without an older female to look after me."

"Those are the normal rules governing the behavior of young women like yourself, Miss de Vere," said the Duke with half a smile. "But it is thought quite safe to let a lady be driven in the Park, when the gentleman has a pair of horses to manage. Besides," he added haughtily, "my place in society is such that many rules that apply to other men do not have to be observed by myself. Let me tell you, Miss de Vere, that if I am seen to be taking an interest in you, it will do you no harm whatsoever. Indeed, it will do the reverse. It will bring you into fashion immediately."

Clorinda hardly knew what to say to this. She tried to look coolly amused but only managed to look charmingly muddled.

Just at that moment, a small child ran in front of the galloping horses in pursuit of his hoop. The Duke, scarcely checking them, swerved to avoid the toddler, then swerved back to avoid an imminent collision with another phaeton.

"You drive much too fast," said Clorinda severely, clutching the sides of her seat.

"You are not very polite, Miss de Vere," said the Duke laughing aloud. "I am not entirely used to receiving so many harsh words from females. They are generally more obliging to me than you are. First you refuse to tell me who you are, even after I have rescued you from Lord Winterstoke. Then you accuse me of being a bad driver."

"I suppose I ought to be polite to you," said Clorinda reluctantly. "You are obviously very fashionable, even if your way of life is pointless. Indeed you are obviously extremely eligible, too." She wondered whether he would now mention that he was married.

He did nothing of the kind. Instead he retorted, "That much cannot be said for Jack de Villiers. He is extremely ineligible, and his way of life is even more pointless than mine. I have not gambled away my fortune, as that young man would do, if he only had a fortune with which to do it. You would be well advised not to jaunter round the town with him, Miss de Vere. I imagine you were with him last night at Vauxhall Gardens, and with the Willoughby boy and his wife. Willoughby seems a sound enough boy, but I think I should warn you about Sir Jack de Villiers."

Clorinda was outraged. Who did he think he was? "I have known Jack and his sister for years," she said with perfect truth. "Why, we were practically brought up together. He and I are like brother and sister."

"The intimacy of a shared childhood might easily lead to the intimacy of marriage," said the Duke grimly. "It does not make up for the fact that Sir Jack de Villiers is both poverty stricken and a reckless gambler."

"He comes from an excellent family. The de Villiers are worthy of an alliance with the foremost in the land." Clorinda longed to add that she knew he, the Duke, had thought the family worth marrying into. Surely now he would reveal his marriage?

But all he said was, "No amount of good breeding can make up for being married to a gambler and a man without money. Unless, Miss de Vere, you have a fortune with which to endow your husband, you would be well advised to look for a more wealthy young man as a companion.

"Poverty is difficult to bear. It is the way of the world to try and make sure that young and romantic ladies do not recklessly throw themselves into it."

"It is a hateful world which makes people marry for money," said Clorinda hotly. Too hotly. For a second she was afraid that her vehemence would have given her away.

But to her surprise the Duke said quite seriously to her: "Perhaps it is a hateful world in this respect. But there is *some* good in its rules. If you are guided by me, Miss de Vere, you will avoid Sir Jack de Villiers. Oh, I know he has charm and energy, but I believe he would make any woman unhappy who linked her life and her fortunes with his."

Clorinda could not help silently admitting the truth of all this. It was unpleasant, but it could not be denied that Jack, though he might be idolized by his sisters, was a reckless gambler and a scapegrace. But she did not admit any of this aloud to the Duke. She was too angry. Why did he take it upon himself to talk to her like this?

"Why should *I* be guided by *you*, Your Grace?" she cried. "You seem to think that your rank as a Duke gives you the right to order everybody about!"

"I know what I am talking about. Besides, my rank certainly does give me privileges, and only an innocent, such as yourself, would deny this," replied the Duke

"Ten years of being chased by matchmakers have made me decide that my rank and my fortune will serve to conceal any faults in my personality. To the mothers of unmarried daughters I am perfection —whatever I do.

"If an ordinary gentleman is rude, he is condemned: I am excused by being called 'original.' If I flirt outrageously with their daughters, then the Mamas merely say that I am high-spirited. If I were a half-pay officer, those same daughters would be severely told to have nothing to do with me. Because I am a Duke, I can flirt as much as I like.

"I assure you, Miss de Vere, that because I am a Duke I can behave like a groom and still be welcome everywhere."

"Just because everybody else toadeats you, doesn't mean that I am going to start," said Clorinda indignantly. "I am grateful for your help last night, but I still think you are arrogant when you presume to give me advice. Still," and she added the insult deliberately, "I suppose you are so much older than me, that your advice is meant to be fatherly. So perhaps I should take it in that spirit."

"My dear girl, I am hardly that old," said the Duke with a surprised look on his face.

Clorinda got the impression she was the first female ever to say something rude to him. Determined to see how far she could go, she continued, "Perhaps you are not old in years, but your behavior is so formal and sober that it is not the behavior of a young man, more of a man in his middle years."

The Duke's face was a picture of astonishment. For a second it looked as if he was going to administer a brutal snub. But all he said was, "Will you be attending the Prince Regent's ball at Carlton House, Miss de Vere?"

"I hope so, Your Grace," replied Clorinda with

demure and equal formality. "Why should it concern you?"

"I shall dance with you on that occasion," said the Duke abruptly, abandoning his usual languid drawl.

"You will not," retorted Clorinda furiously. "Has it never occurred to you that I may not want to dance with you? Or do you expect me to behave like the young ladies you say flirt with you so outrageously?"

"Miss de Vere, think again," said the Duke smoothly. Clorinda had the impression that he was fencing with her. "Think how a dance with me will help you in your career as a fashionable beauty? You may not wish to dance with me, but can you afford to refuse? If you are seen to suit my discriminating taste, then the rest of the world will follow my example."

The arrogance of his words almost made Clorinda lose control. With a heroic effort she managed to rein back her temper. The Duke was insufferable. She longed to throw his offer of a dance back in his teeth. But it was not part of her plans. Better to dance with him—and by this means enslave him!

"Now that you have explained this," she said with a passable imitation of his smooth manner, "I see you are right. I may not wish to dance with you, but I must bear with the boredom of it in pursuit of fashion. I shall be delighted therefore to dance with you, Your Grace. Are you going to bring me into fashion, as I am told you have brought Lady Lancaster?"

"That is a very foolish remark, Miss de Vere," said the Duke coldly. "It is quite improper that a young girl scarcely out of the nursery like yourself should like my name with that of Lady Lancaster."

"All London links your name with hers," retorted Clorinda. "I am only surprised that you will admit your friendship with her is an improper one."

From the look on the Duke's face, Clorinda could see that she had struck home. He was scowling with real anger. "I do not understand why you are so singular, Miss de Vere," he sneered. "Are you attempting to make me notice you? Is this a novel form of feminine pursuit?"

Clorinda was almost speechless with fury. It seemed he effortlessly assumed every woman was out to catch him. "Does it never cross your mind, Duke, that perhaps some women are *not* charmed by you. Has it not occurred to you that my conversation may simply be an ordinary response to a rude manner by yourself?"

"Miss de Vere," he said, "what does occur to me is that you are an impertinent chit."

"And you, Sir, are an arrogant rake," she flung back at him.

Mercifully the matched grays had almost circled round the Park by now. The rest of their progress was accomplished in silence. Both occupants of the phaeton were past speaking with fury.

Just before they cantered up to Emily and Jack who had strolled to meet them, the Duke achieved outward calm. In a voice that was both formal and cold he said, "I hope you have enjoyed being behind my grays, Miss de Vere."

"I have, indeed. They are wonderful horses." There was just enough emphasis in her voice to make it clear that she could not approve of their owner in the same way. Then, to provoke him further, she added in a soulful, insincere voice, "How ravishing the Park looks at this time of year. How charming the flowers are, how delightful is the shade from the trees . . ."

The Duke did not respond. Only a twitch at the corner of that sneering mouth showed that he realized the apparently innocent remarks were meant as provocation. By the time they drew up with Emily and Jack, Clorinda had praised the Duke's horses again, asked if there was much company in London, expressed her pleasure in the sunlight, and wondered if the weather would stay so fine. The Duke had said nothing to the flow of small talk.

If the Duke hope to punish her with his formality, thought Clorinda, well she would show him how she would not accept it submissively. Besides, the man beside her might be tiresome but the weather *was* fine, and the occasion was delightful. She also could not help noticing that her appearance behind the grays had created a great deal of interest. Several young bucks had ogled her shamelessly and some sophisticated matrons had looked at her with approving interest.

It was irritating to think that perhaps the Duke's undoubted arrogance was based on the truth. Perhaps—just perhaps—he was right. Perhaps he *could* bring her into fashion just by noticing her.

As the phaeton came to a halt, and the waiting groom ran to the horses' heads, she climbed gingerly down from her seat, her color heightened at the thought of having to tell Emily about the conversation during their ride.

The Duke nodded formal acknowledgements to Jack, and leaning down to Emily said, "As Miss de Vere's chaperon, I thought you might like to know

125

that she has promised me a dance at the Prince Regent's ball."

"We shall look forward to seeing you there," said Emily gently. She was surprised to receive a burning look of reproach from her sister, and an almost equally angry glance from the Duke. With a sneering laugh, he drove off, the groom scrambling up beside him just in time.

"I must say his manners are sometimes far from pleasing," said Emily plaintively. "What did I say that was wrong?"

"I did not promise him a dance at all. Indeed I said he shouldn't assume I wanted to dance with him, and that the only reason why I would was because he could bring me into fashion," stormed Clorinda. "He is unbelievably arrogant."

"Been fighting with him, have you?" said Jack knowingly. "I thought you had. With your color all high, I knew it. Some people might think you'd been flirting, but I could see not. What a fierce girl you are, Clorinda. If you want to captivate your Duke, should you not try for a gentler manner with him? You'll scare him off, I tell you."

"We were fighting over *you* among other things. He had the impertinence, the absolutely absurd impertinence, to warn me against you. He said you were a gambler, and not a fit companion for a well brought up girl. It was insufferable, Jack. Oh yes, and he said you would not make me happy if I married you."

"He's absolutely right," said Jack amiably. "Can't think why you found the need to quarrel. After all, Clorinda, I wouldn't let you marry me . . . I mean, if you could, which you can't anyway. Well, what I mean is that no sister of mine would be allowed to marry me, though I suppose I wouldn't be your brother, if you could, so I wouldn't have any say in it."

"Oh, Jack, do stop talking rubbish," said Clorinda in exasperation. "It's all quite beside the point. It may be true you're a gambler and so on. But the point is that he has not got the right to dictate to me. He's not my brother. He's not even my suitor. He's a married man with a wife in the country and just because he's a Duke, doesn't mean he can go round warning girls about you."

Jack was about to explain to his sister that perhaps the Duke had a point, but he thought better of it. "Phew, you are a firebrand today," was all he said. "The Duke must have been amazed. Know what? I think he may have taken a dislike to you after this?"

"It's all very well for you to say you wouldn't let your sister marry somebody like yourself," she retorted, "but why did you let me marry the Duke?"

There was an awkward pause. As they strolled on, Clorinda, her heart softening, saw that her brother's face had reddened. It was unusual for him to look conscience-stricken, but this time he did.

In a completely changed voice, he said, "Clorinda, I know that I was wrong to consent to your being the family sacrifice. I should never have let you marry the Duke. You were just too young, and that was all there was to it.

"But we were all in such a devil of a fix that I could see no other way out of our difficulties. You must believe I thought it was for the best," he pleaded. "The Duke is rich and handsome, and I thought perhaps he might make a good husband. I had no idea he would behave so unfeelingly to you, and that it would turn out like this."

Before Clorinda had time to reply to this, they were interrupted by greetings from a sophisticatedly dressed woman in a landau. She looked familiar to Clorinda, but she couldn't think where or when she had met her.

"Jack," commanded the landau's elegant occupant, "you must make me known to the young ladies you are escorting."

After she had been introduced, she nodded politely to Emily. "I heard of your marriage, my dear, though we have never met. May I welcome you to London. I hope you will be coming to my rout next week—nothing grand. Just a few friends."

Somewhat overpowered by this distinguishing attention from an older matron, for the lady in the landau was middle-aged, Emily said softly, "I should be delighted."

"Bring Miss de Vere with you. Now don't forget I expect you both. I dare say I shall have a lot more young men attending, if it's known she's attending. Unusual kind of beauty—but the Duke's detected it already I see. All the rage, I dare swear, in a week or two."

After this embarrassing and rather rude speech, she ordered her carriage to drive on. "Who on earth is she?" asked Clorinda in a bewildered tone of voice. "She seems somehow familiar but I can't place her."

"Oh that's Lady Claremont," said Jack off-handedly. "Didn't you meet her at your wedding, Clorinda? She's an eccentric but in the top of society and a cousin or something to the Duke.

"She must think you're his latest flirt. It's an

honor to be asked to her house. Must be because she's decided the Duke is going to bring you into fashion."

Clorinda couldn't help feeling elated. The way of the fashionable world *was* hateful, if you looked at it from the outside. But from the inside it was so thrilling.

One moment she had been the unloved child bride in the country, deserted by her husband for the sophisticated charms of Lady Lancaster. Now suddenly she was taking her place in polite society. From being an unknown looked down upon, it seemed she was going to be all the rage.

Her pleasure in this was only marred by the undoubted fact that she owed all this to the Duke, and to the drive in his phaeton. He had boasted he could bring her into fashion. It seemed as if his boast was justified.

But she could not feel angry for long. She was only seventeen, and life was just too thrilling. A group of young officers were the next ones to halt and talk to Jack. One of them, being introduced to the two girls, devoted himself to them both.

His name was Lord Rudolph Chiltern, he told them, and he was just on leave from his soldierly duties with the Guards regiment. He had an amusing way of poking fun at himself. He told the girls, with mock seriousness, that he was completely idle and ne'er-do-well, but, did they not agree, he was a social asset.

His banter amused Clorinda. She was also fascinated to see that Jack got on so well with the other officers. "I didn't know that Jack had so many friends who were Army men," she said, forgetting how familiar it was to use just his first name in front of a stranger who did not know they were brother and sister.

"Oh, he's mad about the Army. Knows all Wellington's victories. Lectures us all on Marlborough's tactics. We joke with him and say he'll be joining the ranks as a private next, taking the King's shilling..."

Looking at Jack, Clorinda realized her informant was speaking the truth. Surrounded by the officers, he was discussing the exact use of artillery, drawing diagrams on the sand of Rotten Row with a stick, and arguing nineteen to the dozen. She wondered why she had never before realized where his real interest lay. Somehow she would have to get him a commission in the Army—perhaps the Duke would pay for one.

"Known Jack long, Miss de Vere?" said Lord Chiltern politely but with distinct curiosity.

"Yes, I have," she said with apparent frankness. "I have been a close friend of the family for years. Jack and I are practically brother and sister." It seems as if she would have to say this to almost everybody. Really, it was more awkward than she had bargained for.

"Oh it's you, Winterstoke." Lord Chiltern's voice held no warmth, as he turned round to see who had joined the party. To her consternation, Clorinda realized that this was the man who had drunkenly tried to ... kiss her in Vauxhall gardens. She felt herself blushing and angrily tried to cool her hot cheeks, as he was introduced.

There was nothing she could say in public, she decided.

"I think, if I am not mistaken, that I have already met Miss de Vere," Lord Winterstoke was saying with complete lack of shame or embarrassment. Indeed, as he spoke, his eyes roved over her body greedily, and she found herself clutching her pelisse more tightly round her.

For an appalling moment she thought he was going to reveal the circumstances of their meeting, but he did not, only smiling when Lord Chiltern said jovially, "Lucky dog, Winterstoke. I see you've stolen a march on me. I've only just managed to make Miss de Vere's acquaintance."

"I hope I shall get to know Miss de Vere much better," said the older man and his words were insolent. Clorinda knew that he was thinking of that moment in the dark alleyway when his lips had gone down upon hers . . .

"We'll all want to know Miss de Vere better," Lord Chiltern's cheery voice broke in on her embarrassment. Clorinda knew that he was only flirting. His confession of being a "ne'er-do-well" was tantamount to a confession that he was not in search of a wife. But she liked him the more for that honesty.

She felt that Lord Chiltern's compliments disguised a genuine kindness and a merry nature. The smoothly practiced remarks of Lord Winterstoke were something different . . . She smiled at Lord Chiltern, imperceptibly turning her shoulder a little upon Lord Winterstoke.

"Shall you be at the Prince Regent's ball, Lord Chiltern?" she asked.

"I shall," he said promptly. "Dare I hope that you will dance the waltz with me? And," he said, showing his good manners by including Emily in the conversation, "I hope I shall have Robert Willoughby's permission to dance with his delightful wife.

You two ladies will outshine all the other beauties there."

"I should love that," said Clorinda unselfconsciously.

"Shall you love a dance with me?" The unwelcome question came from Lord Winterstoke. Once again, Clorinda thought that he looked old—rakishly, dissippatedly and disgustingly old.

She bowed stiffly to him, not trusting herself to speak.

"Of course, now that the Duke of Westhampton has shown such an interest in your charms Miss de Vere, us lesser mortals may not be able to aspire to your hand." His every word was a sneer.

"Yes, by Jove," Lord Chiltern seemed unaware of the older man's sarcasm. "Too bad of Westhampton. You know that he's been driving Miss de Vere in his phaeton today? It's unheard of, Miss de Vere. He's never had a female up beside him before, you know? The beauties will be gnashing their teeth with rage at you when this gets round society."

"Really?" said Clorinda coldly. "It was amusing for a moment to be driven by the Duke. But I find I do not care for it as much as I might. In this respect, gentlemen, I fear I shall be classed as unfashionable. I find I have little time for a 'leader of fashion' like the Duke."

"You're too stern, Miss de Vere," said Lord Chiltern slightly bewildered.

"Perhaps Miss de Vere finds the Duke *mal adroit?*" sneered Lord Winterstoke. "He is known for his arrogant interference."

With this parting shot he lounged off, casually lifting his hat to Emily, and ignoring Jack altogether with a drawling, "Au revoir, ladies. We shall meet at the Carlton House ball."

"I hope you will forgive me for saying this," said Lord Chiltern diffidently, "but Winterstoke is a bit of a rake. Shouldn't say so of course, and have no right to, but you ought to know." Then, saving the girls embarrassment, he rattled on with compliments and stories that kept them amused till at last Jack extracted himself from the military discussion and offered his arm to his sisters.

"Don't you encourage that fellow Winterstoke," he said to Clorinda when they had said goodbye to Lord Chiltern. "I wonder if I ought to warn him off my sister?"

"He's your gambling crony," said Clorinda bitterly. "I certainly haven't given him any encouragement. I think he's a disgusting old man. But I can't stop him from introducing himself in the Park."

"Yes, really Jack, Clorinda was very off-hand with him."

"Perhaps I had better see less of Winterstoke while you are here," said Jack. Clorinda was pleased to see that he was frowning a little. Obviously, while he found Lord Winterstoke amusing for himself, he was not prepared to let the notorious rake get involved with females of his family. It was a good sign, thought Clorinda, that Jack might take on some responsibility, after all.

"Lord Chiltern was very attentive. We like him," offered Emily in an attempt to lighten Jack's mood.

"Chiltern's a gentleman and a good fellow. You won't come to harm with him, Clorinda," said Jack. "But what worries me is where is this all going to end? Now that the Duke has shown in public that he's interested, everybody's going to want to find out about this Miss de Vere. And what are we going to tell them, Emily? It'll be a mystery soon."

"This is just what I want," said Clorinda. "I want to be a mystery, a girl who has arrived from nowhere. When the Duke sees how other men find me attractive, perhaps he will fall in love with me himself. And then I shall know that he loves me for myself, not for my family or my background."

"That's all very well, but what'll happen next? I've been thinking about it," said Jack unexpectedly. "Seems to me that we've let ourselves in for a lot more trouble and deception than we thought. How are we going to explain to the fashionable world that you were the Duchess all along? What will Lady Claremont think, for one?"

"I'm sure we'll manage somehow," said Clorinda. "The Duke was awfully rude to me but he did take me up in his phaeton and Lord Chiltern says that it's the first time he's driven a female. Perhaps he is captivated after all."

"Unless he's doing it just to be eccentric," said Jack dampeningly. "Everybody knows that there's nothing Westhampton likes better than leading the fashionable world by the nose every now and again."

"Wait till the Prince Regent's ball," said Emily. "Clorinda is going to amaze everybody with her beauty. What is Madame Latour making for you?"

The two girls fell to discussing muslins and flounces and the rival merits of ribbon colors, so that Jack whistled a tune rudely all the way home, complaining that he had never in all his life been so bored by a conversation.

After he had left, Clorinda remembered what Lord Chiltern had said. "Do you think Jack should have been in the Army, rather than simply lounging around London?" she asked her sister.

"Perhaps I should have stayed back at Westhampton and waited for the Duke?" she said worriedly. "He might have bought Jack a commission in the Army, if I had asked him at a favorable moment."

Then she thought of her drive with the Duke. She gave a little chuckle as she remembered the Duke's scowling face when she had mentioned Lady Lancaster.

"Perhaps I shall win this battle with him after all," she said to herself. "Perhaps the dowdy Clorinda de Villiers will conquer the great and powerful Duke of Westhampton."

(7)

It was a ball gown that would have graced a fairy princess.

Over a perfect white satin which gleamed and caught the light, Madame Genevieve had draped a silvery gauze material. At the hem, the edge of the little puffed sleeves, and at the top of the low cut bodice, drawn silver thread work embroidery discreetly gathered up the gauzy folds.

The most cunning touch of all, however, were the tiny seed pearls scattered like teardrops among the embroidery. The whole effect was that of a silvery cloud, misty and mysterious, sparkling with little raindrops.

Clorinda, however, felt uncertain. "It makes me look rather young," she said, a note of dismay creeping into her voice as she stood in front of the large mirror with its gilt cupids and flowers framing her. "I am afraid the Duke will think I am just . . . a young girl."

She was right in her perceptions. As never before, the strangely silver material outlined her immaturity. If the Eau de Nil dress had made her look like a woman, this gave her a strange ethereal quality, an other-worldliness.

Madame Latour simply smiled at Clorinda's criticism. "Lady Lancaster, she is older, is she not?" she said. "You must not try to fight fire with fire, little one. You have what she has not, and can now never have, which is innocence and youth. Of a surety, she would give her all to recapture what this dress makes so clear in you.

"Trust me," she added. "I know a little about the ways of men. Sometimes one must excite them, but sometimes it is necessary to make them adore. This is a dress to create adoration."

Clorinda sighed, and decided she would trust the Frenchwoman's taste. Beside, there was no more time. The great ball at Carlton House was for tonight. She had taxed the resources of Madame Latour's establishment to their utmost to get the dress finished at all.

"And now, the final touches." Madame Latour produced tiny satin dancing shoes, which Clorinda saw had the same little pearls sewn on them. Pointing each toe in turn before the mirror, Clorinda admitted that they were delightful.

"They are almost like Cinderella's glass slippers," she said joyfully.

As she spoke, Monsieur Lafayette let himself into the room. She turned toward him, and displayed to him a deep and dignified manner in what he called a *grande dame* style. Then happily she danced over to him.

He took the hand which she held out and raised it to his lips. His eyes in their deep sockets smiled at her, "*Eh bien,* my lesson has not been wasted. I could almost wish I too was a visitor at this most magnificent of balls. You have done well, Genevieve. She looks like a Diana, a virginal goddess of the moon. I am glad to have seen her thus before I retire."

"Where are you going?" asked Clorinda with interest.

"It is my custom to spend most of my days in a small cottage in Little Repton," he said. "Since I have adjured society, I attempt to find my peace of mind in my garden there. It is not far from Westhampton, my child. It is a countryside which reminds me of happier days, days that I cannot recollect without regret."

"Perhaps you will come and visit me at Westhampton?" said Clorinda tentatively. She was dismayed that the old French aristocrat was leaving London. "If my plan does not succeed I shall be very lonely there. I shall need a friend," she added pathetically.

"You shall visit me, my dear," said the old man. "Remember I am always your friend and you can come any time. And perhaps if your plan succeeds and you ask the Duke's permission, I might visit Westhampton once again."

"You have been there before?" Clorinda was surprised.

"Many times but so long ago," said Monsieur Lafayette in a tone of deepest nostalgia. "Now that you see me as an old man living retired, you cannot imagine that I was once a gallant, as fashionable as your Duke. Before the Revolution tore my country apart, I visited Westhampton—and lost my heart.

"I did a great wrong for love in those days. But I was punished. I hope that perhaps through you I can restore some love and gaiety to Westhampton.

But this is too long a tale to explain now. Be happy, my child. Come, let me try your waltz."

It was an odd sight. The elegant old aristocrat, all in black, and the ravishingly beautiful young girl in a cloud of white silver, circling the salon to the sounds of imaginary music. And they came to a halt, Monsieur Lafayette bent down to the small figure in his embrace, and kissed her gently on the forehead.

"I am not the Prince who shall awake this sleeping beauty, but allow me the privilege of a man old enough to be your father, my dear," he said gently.

It seemed to Clorinda that this gesture of his was somehow a blessing. For a moment she had the oddest thought that perhaps her journey in search of love was partly undertaken on behalf of others—this strange couple, the old French aristocrat who had lost the woman he loved in mysterious circumstances, and the charming French woman whose life had been ruined by a ruthless deceiving man.

"You have both been very kind to me," she said wonderingly. "I do not really know why."

"Perhaps it is because we see our old selves in you," said Madame Genevieve, as if she had read Clorinda's earlier thought. "We have lost the loves that we most valued. Perhaps we, too, have a debt to repay because we did not love wisely, though we loved well. We cannot be but sympathetic to those who are still in search of what their heart demands. Listen to your heart, Clorinda. It is a dangerous thing, but only a heart can lead you to happiness. Good fortune, my little one," she added, and she too kissed Clorinda as she said goodby.

Back at Emily's house, Clorinda discovered that she had missed more social activity. Lord Winterstoke had apparently called, and she was happy that she had missed him. He had only stayed a few minutes when he discovered she was not there and had barely been civil to Emily.

Lord Chiltern had then followed him, and was still there entertaining her sister with outrageous compliments and amusing anecdotes about high society.

"Look what he has brought you," said Emily excitedly. "They are perfectly wonderful flowers."

It was a huge bouquet of scented white roses, that were already filling the drawing room with their delicious fragrance. Each flower was only just uncurling its petals. A large white satin ribbon tied so that it made a treble bow held the flowers.

Clorinda picked them up and buried her tilted little nose into their blooms. "They are simply divine," she said appreciatively. "But I must give them to the butler to put in water immediately before they fade."

She had an idea. "I would like to make a wreath for my hair out of them tonight—if you would agree, Lord Chiltern. They are so perfect that they will exactly match my new gown."

"Miss de Vere, if you wear my roses in your hair tonight at the Carlton House ball, I shall positively expire with delight. Life will have no more exquisite pleasure for me," said Lord Chiltern. Only a twinkle in his eye robbed the compliment of its extravagance.

"You know," said Clorinda seriously, though she could not help blushing too. "I should like you so much more if you didn't say these silly things . . ."

Lord Chiltern laughed. "To most ladies compliments are not only delightful, they are essential."

Turning to Emily he said, and his eyes were kind, "Your friend is an original. I have never met anybody like her."

As Clorinda handed his bouquet to the butler, she could not help asking him, "Were there no other callers?"

"No, Miss de Vere," was the reply.

So the Duke had not bothered to call. Perhaps Jack had been right, and his grace had not cared for her frankness in Hyde Park. Lord Chiltern said she was an original, and he liked it. But perhaps the Duke cared for more conventional beauties. "Like Lady Lancaster," her heart whispered bitterly.

Lord Chiltern's flowers turned out not to be the only ones that Clorinda received that day. As she was dressing for the ball, two more arrived. One was a huge spray of hot house orchids, curiously shaped and in weird colors. Clorinda was not sure if she really liked these exotic flowers, though she knew that they must have cost a fabulous sum of money. With them came a card which read "In hope of a closer friendship and in admiration of your charms." It was signed by Lord Winterstoke.

The other bouquet was much more simple. It was more of a posy than a bouquet. The flowers were small wild lilies, of a kind that are sometimes found in hidden meadows. The card with it bore just the one word—"Westhampton."

"I do not think the orchids will look suitable on you," said her sister. "But either the roses or the lilies will look perfect in a wreath. Perhaps you'd better wear the lilies since they are sent by the Duke. I wonder where he got them?"

"I shall wear the roses," said Clorinda promptly. "They are nicer than the orchids, and the lilies are too fragile, I think. Besides it will be good for the Duke to see I have not worn his flowers."

"Sometimes I wonder about you," said Emily in a puzzled voice. "You say you want to make the Duke fall in love with you, Clorinda, but why? Sometimes I think that you hate him and that it's all just for revenge."

Her sister blushed. Emily's words made her feel uncomfortable. "It is just that I think the Duke is insufferably conceited," she said in excuse. "And anyway I told Lord Chiltern that I would wear his roses."

Carlton House, itself, was amazing. The Prince Regent had literally spent a fortune on it. Over and over again he had run into debt—and a large part of these debts had been because of Carlton House, and later his Pavilion at Brighton.

The furniture for the house alone had cost one hundred and sixty thousand pounds according to one estimate. The drawing room had been decorated in Chinese fashion with Chinese furniture. The coverings for this had cost almost seven thousand pounds and another four hundred pounds or so had been spent on oil lanterns to light it.

Clorinda was bewildered by the magnificence of it all. The ballroom was decorated with rich hangings and huge banks of flowers. Iced champagne was available everywhere, carried by flunkies dressed in dark blue liveries with trimmings of gold lace.

It seemed to her that she had never before seen gathered together so many glittering people. As well as beautiful women, in every color and design of dress, flashing with jewels in their hair, there were dashing Army officers in the full glory of their regimental colors, exotic-looking ambassadors from foreign countries ablaze with medals on their chests, and even the occasional Indian rajah in a jeweled turban. Even Jack and Robert halted for a moment on the threshold of the ballroom, dazzled by the sight of so many silks, jewels and other finery.

Then she saw the Duke. He was simply dressed, wearing a black coat, severely plain, with only a single diamond pin at the neck of his cravat. His neck cloth, indeed, was innocent of lace, but, this time, of a dazzlingly intricate pattern so that it fell rather like a waterfall from his neck.

He was standing by some huge French windows with a woman that Clorinda could recognize as Lady Lancaster. As the Duke had his back toward her, Clorinda could for the first time examine the face of his companion without a mask.

There was no doubt that Lady Lancaster was a beauty of the first order. In a mask she had looked wonderful; without one she looked even better. Her color was marvelous. Jet black hair combined with white skin and red, red lips—like blood on snow, thought Clorinda and could not help but shiver.

Lady Lancaster's beauty was not very warm—hot and fiery perhaps, or cold as ice, but it gave the impression of a woman who was passionate but not kind.

She and the Duke were talking earnestly to each other, ignoring everybody else in the room. Even from across the ballroom, where Clorinda was standing, she could see that their conversation was intense. She sensed that they were discussing their relationship.

While she watched, the Duke stretched out his

hand and laid it—just for a second—upon Lady Lancaster's bare shoulder. The gesture was incredibly intimate. With a shock, Clorinda realized it was the sort of gesture a husband might make to his wife . . . Irrelevantly her mind wandered back to that evening when the Duke had walked past her bedroom door . . .

Whatever it was that lay at the heart of a man and a woman's relationship, obviously the Duke and Lady Landaster had experienced it. Clorinda felt very young.

Then the Duke and his companion looked round the room for a second, and turning their backs on the dancing throng, walked out together, the Duke holding open the French windows' door for the lady.

There was an eager longing upon her face. The Duke's expression was as impassive as ever. For a moment, before the heavy curtains swung back and hid the scene, Clorinda caught a glimpse of Lady Lancaster stretching out her arms to the Duke in an embrace.

Just then Robert Willoughby said to her, "May I have the honor of leading you out for a cotillion?" And Clorinda found herself whisked out onto the gay dancing floor. She performed her part in the dance with grace, but she could see nothing more of that scene by the window.

Had she been able to watch, she might have seen a more than usually white-faced Lady Lancaster storm back into the room through those same velvet curtains. Her face was set in an expression of indescribable fury. Several minutes later, when she had walked off and lost herself in the crowd, the

Duke, as cool as ever, emerged. Nothing could be read in his expression but perhaps a faint touch of his usual languid boredom.

Willoughby was succeeded as Clorinda's partner by Lord Chiltern. "I see that you are wearing my roses," he said sentimentally. "They will never fade, I dare say, after this."

"They are very nice, but may I ask you a more important question. Do you think that Jack would make a good soldier? I only ask this because I am fond of the de Villiers family and therefore have his interests at heart," she said hurriedly in explanation.

"You are pitiless with your admirers, Miss de Vere," mourned Lord Chiltern in mock seriousness. "You ignore their compliments and then you ask them about the interests of other men. What is Jack de Villiers to you?"

Clorinda gave a little peal of laughter. "Lord Chiltern, do not tease me. I have already told you that Jack is a sort of honorary brother to me. That is all."

"Well, Miss de Vere, I can tell you that he would make as good an officer as he makes a bad gambler."

"Thank you, Lord Chiltern," said Clorinda with real gratitude. "That is exactly what I suspected."

As waltz followed waltz and young man after young man swept Clorinda on to the floor, a feeling of light-hearted enjoyment came over her. For the present she forgot all about the Duke, about her deception, and her plans to gain her revenge on him.

She was just a young girl enjoying her first formal dance. Finally when it was Jack's time to partner her, she asked him if he would sit this one out.

He agreed with alacrity, being only too happy to avoid what he called "this capering on the dance floor." While she stood and fanned herself, he went in search of a glass of lemonade for her.

"Miss de Vere, I have come to claim my dance," said a voice beside her. It was Lord Winterstoke.

"Excuse me, Lord Winterstoke. I think you have made an error," said Clorinda haughtily. "I owe this dance to Jack de Villiers who has kindly gone to fetch me some lemonade."

"His absence is my opportunity, fairest one," said the sneering tones of the middle-aged rake. He made as if to put his hand about her waist.

A heavy grasp on his shoulders stopped him in his tracks. Looking down on him was the Duke. "You are both mistaken," he said with authority. "This is my dance. I am ashamed that you have forgotten it, Miss de Vere."

Thankful to have avoided Lord Winterstoke, but angry at the Duke's confidence, Clorinda nevertheless found herself moving into his arms. It was as if something about the man hypnotized her, she told herself angrily. She could see Winterstoke scowling at the edge of the floor, and Jack looking surprised as he returned with the lemonade.

She did not care. It was as if she was powerless to resist the Duke's summons.

The waltz was even more thrilling than the one she had danced with him at Vauxhall Gardens. This time she was unmasked, so was he. It made the experience more naked. She thought that perhaps she was held more closely in his arms, but perhaps this was just her imagination.

She knew that all around her people were commenting on the fine couple they made—the girl in white, the imperious Duke in black. She was conscious throughout the whirling dance, of his strong arms about her, holding her up, guiding her through the intricacies of the steps. She could also feel—and the thought made her blush—his strong body behind them, close to hers.

She had been enjoying the dancing, but this was something magically different. It was as though they, two, were in perfect harmony in a world where everything was everybody else was out of step. It was as though the music had obliterated self in an ecstatic communion of two souls.

At the back of her mind Clorinda was dimly conscious that this was silent rapture. She knew she should have been making light-hearted conversation of the sort she enjoyed with Lord Chiltern. She knew that he might think her naive or rude or awkward because she did not speak.

But what she was experiencing with the Duke was too deep for words. The moments of the waltz seemed almost sacred. It was as though they were ascending into a heaven of music and rhythm.

It was like coming down to earth when the music stopped. To her surprise she found herself being led off the floor by the Duke, who also remained silent. They threaded their way through the throng of fashionable people smiling and bowing and making remarks.

Clorinda felt in a dream. The magic moments of the waltz were still in her heart.

As they left the room behind them, the Duke finally spoke. His voice was low and urgent. "I must talk to you. I shall go mad unless I do."

He led her into a small room where a card table

148

had been set up, but where there was nobody playing.

They were completely alone. The Duke did not shut the door, perhaps because he knew that would compromise Clorinda utterly. Through it, she could see the dance proceeding without them.

With a little blind gesture, she shook her head. She *must* think. Now was the moment, perhaps, when the Duke should be undone by her captivating charm.

She was more than a little frightened, as she faced him. But she schooled herself to smile. Like somebody in a dream, she fluttered her long lashes at him, shyly half glancing up at him with what she hoped was a provocative look.

Suddenly she was in his arms . . . unselfconsciously she tilted her face toward his, as a flower bends upward toward the rays of the sun. His lips touched hers, gently as the flutter of a butterfly's wing. Her breath almost stopped at that first magic contact.

Then his mouth came down on hers harder, and closer, and more demanding. She could see his eyes blazing with passion, as he drew her close to him. She could feel the buttons of his black coat pressing into her.

She knew she ought to struggle against his embrace . . . that this was wrong . . . but she could not. Her breath was coming in quick pants, while she could feel him breathing as if he had been running. She was very conscious of his bodily strength, but that was not the reason she did not pull back against his arms.

She groaned inwardly. She realized that her

own body was consenting to his unspoken demand. She would do anything for him . . . with a little, half muffled cry, she returned his kiss and melted into his strong arms.

Abruptly and cruelly he tore his lips away from hers, thrusting her rudely from him. "This is folly," he said sternly. "Go back to the ball room." For the space of what must have been only a second, but seemed like an age, Clorinda stood dumbly there, bewildered, unable to take in those brutal words.

But as she was about to plead with him, an angry female voice broke in on them. "Why don't you introduce me to your new friend, Julian?"

It was Lady Lancaster.

She stood there in the doorway, her breast heaving with rage, so that the rich diamonds on it glinted in the candlelight. Her mouth was a snarl of indignation, and her magnificent eyes were flashing with fury.

Unconsciously the Duke made a movement toward Clorinda, as if he would take her back into his arms for protection. Then he checked himself. "You had better go," he repeated. His voice was expressionless now.

Clorinda turned from him to leave, but Lady Lancaster barred the way. "No, stay, you common little flirt," she said cruelly. "Do you think I don't know that you were the girl at Vauxhall Gardens, and that Julian kissed you in the bushes. I suppose you pursued him here in search of more?"

Clorinda said nothing. She was frozen to the ground with horror. This was like a bad dream. She looked imploringly at the Duke and said to him, "I cannot leave."

With an effort the Duke seemed to stop himself from looking at her. He walked straight by her, and pushed rudely past Lady Lancaster. "This is no place for a dramatic scene," he said to her quietly. "Let us leave this place and Miss de Vere in it with dignity. Come, I shall escort you back to the ballroom."

His intervention seemed to enrage Lady Lancaster further. "As always you would do anything to avoid a scene, Julian. You are quite content to play the rake, but always anxious to stay discreet so that nobody knows about it.

"Do you think I haven't known about your opera dancers, and the singer in Vienna, and the Frenchwoman? And now it is my turn, I suppose. Am I to be cast aside like an old glove, once you have wearied of me? Am I to be pensioned off like those other women?

"I warn you, Julian." Her voice was passionate, low and throbbing with emotion. She seemed to temporarily have forgotten Clorinda. "You cannot treat me like you have treated the others."

He took absolutely no notice of what she was saying. Instead he bowed ironically to her and remained silent.

"Go then, Your Grace the oh-so-honorable Duke of Westhampton. I shall never forgive you . . . never, never, never."

The Duke walked calmly away back into the ballroom. Clorinda heard his steps retreating. He was just walking out. He was utterly deserting her without a backward glance. She was left face-to-face with her rival—a rival maddened with rage.

Lady Lancaster tossed her black raven locks. Then she smiled. It was not a pleasant smile. It was more like seeing a tiger licking its lips in anticipation of prey, thought Clorinda, than a smile on the face of a fashionable woman.

"Shall I enlighten your innocence about the Duke?" said Lady Lancaster. She was almost purring. "Shall I tell you the nature of my relationship with his Grace?"

"I already know," said Clorinda, her eyes firmly on the floor.

"You know, and yet you kissed him? What a sophisticated young girl you are." Lady Lancaster was now frankly playing with Clorinda as a cat plays with a bird it has caught. There seemed no escape. She stood firmly in the doorway.

"But perhaps you do not know about the Duke, himself? He has had many mistresses you know, my dear, but few so well-born as myself. No, his usual tastes are more vulgar. Till myself, he frequented muslin company, those beautiful but frail young women who have more beauty than birth.

"Or perhaps you thought he meant marriage?" she continued. "Perhaps you aspired to the Duke's hand, thinking I should not rival you there. If you thought you were going to be successful, I must tell you that you have been fearfully misled.

"Indeed, I might almost say that you are too late, my dear. Did the Duke not explain? Has he perhaps hinted that you might be successful? Too bad of him, to hold out lures that are only deceit."

Her hateful voice seemed to go on and on. Clorinda longed to speak back if only to silence the endless stream of malicious remarks.

"At least it is possible that I might be married to the Duke," she burst out. "Unlike you, I am not married to anybody else."

Lady Lancaster paled for a moment and seemed to flinch. Clorinda almost felt sorry for her. But Her Ladyship's glance looked daggers back. Two spots of red glowed on her magnificent cheeks, and for a second Clorinda thought she might be physically attacked tooth and nail by the maddened woman. Never before had she seen such female fury.

Then behind the outraged form of the woman, she caught sight of an unwelcome figure—Lord Winterstoke.

"Well, well, ladies," his sneering voice broke in. "No doubt you are enjoying a delightful conversation about needlework and fashions and other feminine topics. You two have too much in common . . . or hope to have, perhaps?" His words were a question addressed to Clorinda.

"Lady Lancaster has been kind enough to warn me about fashionable rakes," said Clorinda. Her voice trembled but she faced Lord Winterstoke fearlessly looking him straight in the eyes.

Just for a moment an expression of gratitude flitted across Lady Lancaster's face. The older woman looked horribly upset by Lord Winterstoke's arrival and Clorinda guessed that, if she revealed the nature of the scene that had taken place, Lord Winterstoke would use it to torture Lady Lancaster, as well as herself.

Lady Lancaster gave her a speaking look. Her eyes seemed to implore Clorinda's silence.

"You were discussing fashionable rakes? Like the Duke of Westhampton perhaps?" said the objectionable man, every word emphasized with sarcasm.

"There are many fashionable rakes," retorted Clorinda. "I have been told that certain people, mis-

153

informed no doubt, number you among their ranks."

"That is correct." Lady Lancaster seemed to have rallied. She looked a little less magnificent than before, almost tired perhaps. Collecting herself with an effort, she continued. "Our conversation was a spirited one, but not one that need concern you, Lord Winterstoke. Besides I am sure it is time both of us returned to the ballroom."

"Let me lend you each an arm, dear ladies," purred Lord Winterstoke. "It will be a pleasure to escort two such close friends."

As the woman and the girl halted undecided he went on, "Or shall we continue this delightful chat? I am quite happy to remain here, though it reminds me of the old song—*How happy could I be with either, were t'other dear charmer away.* No doubt the Duke of Westhampton would echo my sentiments."

It was impossible to let him continue in this mocking vein, thought Clorinda. "I shall be happy to accept your escort back to the party," she said frigidly.

"And I, too," said Lady Lancaster reluctantly.

It was a strange threesome that made its way back to the ballroom. Across the floor Clorinda saw Jack's eyes start out of his head, as he perceived in whose company she was. He began to hurry over to them, just as Lady Lancaster with a frozen nod of her head took her hand off Lord Winterstoke's arm saying, "It was a pleasure to meet you, Miss de Vere."

Clorinda had the oddest feeling that the words were not entirely insincere—as if Lord Winterstoke's arrival had in some way changed Lady Lancaster's attitude toward herself.

Then Jack hurried up. "Servant, Winterstoke,"

he said with a not entirely convincing attempt at casual ease. "Miss de Vere, I believe, indeed I am sure, that you owe me this dance."

Clorinda was going to take her arm out of Lord Winterstoke's when the sinister peer placed his larger hand over hers. "I shall not relinquish her to you, Sir Jack," he drawled. "Miss de Vere owes me this dance. I am sure she would not like to leave me until we have had the chance to discuss one or two matters. It would be too bad if I found myself repeating what I have seen."

It was a barely concealed threat. Clorinda flushed. Turning to Jack with an imploring gesture, she said, "What Lord Winterstoke says is true. Perhaps I could have the next dance after this one?"

Jack looked worried. "Please, Jack," she pleaded, and he turned away.

"You are on terms of great intimacy with young Jack de Villiers," said Lord Winterstoke unpleasantly.

"I was practically brought up with the de Villiers family." Clorinda replied automatically. "We are more like brother and sister."

This explanation seemed to satisfy him, for he changed tack. "You are also on considerably intimate terms with the Duke of Westhampton," he said.

"You are mistaken," said Clorinda dully, but she could not stop her color rising in her cheeks.

"I can hardly mistake my eyes when I see the Duke leading a lady off the ballroom floor in search of a quiet room where they may be alone together," the smooth voice tormented her. "A lack of discretion, indeed for one so young as yourself, Miss de Vere.

"For it was not only I who noticed. Your departure caught the attention of the lovely Lady Lancaster. What an interesting discussion the three of you must have had together."

"I do not think that what the Duke does is any of your business," said Clorinda. She was not enjoying the waltz. She felt uncomfortable close to the aging rake who had so brutally assaulted her in Vauxhall Gardens. It was as if his hot breath was again on her lips. She kept her eyes firmly on her feet, not liking to look up and see the greedy lust that she feared would be in his eyes. His hot, damp hands tightened unpleasantly around her waist.

"You forget, Miss de Vere, that I take a great interest in *your* welfare," said Lord Winterstoke. "I have no interest in the Duke, save where he interferes with my own interests. He and Lady Lancaster may do as they please, as far as I am concerned. But he may not do as he pleases with *you*.

"I should not like to think that you have been deceived by him. I hope that you do not think he offers marriage."

"I am not deceived," said Clorinda sadly.

"You are not deceived. That means you do not think he offers marriage, and yet you embrace him," said Lord Winterstoke tauntingly. She could not help but notice that for the first time a smile hovered round his wet mouth. It was not a kind smile.

"Now *that* interests me a great deal, Miss de Vere. I had thought perhaps that you were ambitious for marriage, and was therefore reluctant to make you an offer which you might find, shall we say, less than that ambition. But perhaps after all you may find my offer of interest?"

"I do not know what you mean," replied Clorinda, and truly she did not. The words seemed to float in her mind, not staying long enough for her to comprehend them. A wave of misery, so deeply felt as to be almost unbearable, had swept over her.

"Perhaps you do, perhaps not," went on Lord Winterstoke, unrepressed. "How refreshing you are, Miss de Vere. No anger at impropriety? Instead a kind of eager innocence. You have no idea how tempting it is to one of my jaded sensibilities. I see that I must make myself more plain, but now is obviously not the time. May I call on you tomorrow, Miss de Vere?"

Clorinda did not want to see him at all. The expression on her face must have made this clear, for he continued, "Don't refuse me. If you do I might find it necessary to tell my friends of the curious scene I witnessed tonight. I do not think that it would be good for your reputation, Miss de Vere. Nor would it be good for the reputation of the noble Duke of Westhampton."

"You may call on me tomorrow," said Clorinda, defeated. It was all she could do not to fling herself out of his arms and leave the waltz there and then. But she knew that at all costs she must not make a scene. If she showed her distress publicly it might even reflect badly on gentle Emily.

Where was the Duke? At every turn of the waltz she hoped to set eyes on him, but he had vanished.

She was thankful when the interminable waltz came to an end and Lord Winterstoke handed her over to her waiting brother with only a formal thanks. "We had better dance this one," said Jack reluctantly when the music started. "You have done enough already to set the gossips talking tonight."

It was a country dance and so brother and sister were too much concerned with following the steps and taking their part in the figures for any intimate talk.

Afterward, as he led her back to Emily, Jack grumbled, "I thought Lord Winterstoke amusing, but I don't find his pursuit of you so funny. This behavior won't do, Clorinda.

"I have had to spend half the evening looking for you. First I saw you slip away with the Duke and next, devil take me if I don't see you coming back into the room with Lady Lancaster and Lord Winterstoke. If you take my advice, my girl, you'll have nothing to do with either. What romp have you been up to?"

He would have continued his scolding but Emily came up at this moment. Seeing her sister's eyes full of unshed tears, and her face painfully white she acted swiftly. "Now don't bully her, Jack. Clorinda will explain everything tomorrow. It's been a long evening. I for one am tired. I think it is quite time we all went home."

It was a weary and somewhat woe-begone party that made its way back to the Willoughby household. Jack de Villiers was sulking. Clorinda was too emotionally exhausted to say a word more. It was left to Robert and Emily to talk in the carriage on the way back.

At last they arrived, and Clorinda saw that Betty her maid had waited up for her—though she had told the girl there was no need. "You shouldn't have done it," she said as thankfully she found herself alone in the room with the girl. "Thank you so much, Betty dear."

Very soon, tucked in her bed with a shawl put round her shoulders by her faithful maid, Clorinda began to feel slightly better. "Oh Betty," she sighed, "I have been such a silly little fool. I don't think that my famous plan is going to work at all."

"Now then, Your Grace," said the country girl, burring the edges of her words with the local sound of the countryside. " 'Tis best to leave trouble for the morning. After sleep, they say, you will find a way. Let things sort themselves out. It will come all right tomorrow. Tomorrow is another day, remember?"

(8)

In the early morning light of the following day Hyde Park looked like the country, Clorinda decided. She had stolen out of the house while everybody else was still in bed, in search of solitude to think.

In the Park there was nobody fashionable at this time. Instead of dashing bucks on their spirited horses there were only the grooms exercising in Rotten Row, and the occasional troop of private soldiers from the nearby barracks on their troopers.

Where the fashionable ladies and their attendant gentlemen promenaded, there were now only the unfashionable. An occasional City tradesman was walking to his place of business through the green trees. The odd footman hurried by on some errand. One or two housemaids were enjoying a break snatched from work.

Dew glittered on the grass like the diamonds in the tiaras of the night before. The sheep, grazing in the Park to keep the grass short, baa-ed gently. Clorinda could hear a lark singing somewhere above the smokey rooftops of the capital.

There was also the sound of singing from the

milkmaid who kept a small herd of cows in the Park. During the day she sold milk by the mugful to passing gentlemen, exchanging spirited banter with most of them. Now, before the fine beaux were abroad, she was pleasing herself with a melancholy and not altogether proper love-song.

Everything was at peace. "Except my heart," thought Clorinda. As she walked through the dewy grass leaving a trail of footsteps behind on its virgin purity, she unhappily recounted the events of the evening before.

"I am a fool," she told herself bitterly. The Duke was just a fashionable rake. *His* idea of love was dallying with Lady Lancaster, with little opera dancers and singers. Perhaps he had felt the same interest in the silly Miss de Vere, the new arrival in London who had been idiotic enough to show she cared for his kisses.

Falling in love? That wasn't the way to describe the kind of trivial interest he had in women.

"I don't care," thought Clorinda. But as she silently said the words, she knew that she did. She cared passionately, whole-heartedly—agonizingly.

Oh, she had known all along that the Duke was dangerously attractive, but she had not realized just *how* dangerous. Like a moth she had fluttered round the flame, ignorant of its power to destroy her. Now she was being consumed by it. That one kiss had taught her the true state of her heart.

"I am in love," she said aloud to the thrushes and blackbirds who were seeking for worms in the dewy grass. "I am in love and it hurts. How it hurts!" A single tear coursed its way down her cheek.

She must not cry now. Must not weep for the

loss of a foolish dream, a childish bit of make-believe that had deceived her, as much as others. She must be brave. Taking her arms against a sea of troubles, she must learn to smile despite the sobs of her heart. "Well, there's nothing lost but my heart," she said aloud again to comfort herself.

"Pull yourself together, Clorinda de Villiers," she told herself, this time silently. Then she remembered that it was no longer her name. She was no longer a de Villiers. She was the Duchess of Westhampton, one of an honored line of noble ladies.

Her mind went back to the last Duchess, the Duke's mother, that mysterious figure. She had kept a smile on her lips while her portrait was being painted, the picture that hung in the library of Westhampton. But she had been so unhappy that she had eventually run away.

To take her mind off Westhampton, where so soon she would have to return, she tried to think again of the odious Lord Winterstoke. He was a man that she disliked instinctively. Everything about him seemed to sneer at her—and his bold eyes and way of looking her up and down frightened her.

His words to her when she had had that final reluctant dance with him had been ominous. He had more or less been threatening her with blackmail —the threat that he would reveal all about that kiss between her and the Duke.

Well, she would not be blackmailed. She did not care about her reputation. She had nothing to lose now. Now that she had discovered that she had fallen in love with the Duke, nothing else mattered.

Nothing else? There was a matter of dignity. Her plans had gone entirely awry. She had hoped for revenge, hoped that the Duke would fall in love with her, so that she could punish him for his loveless marriage to her.

How silly, how utterly ridiculous had been the result. Instead of gaining her revenge, she had fallen helplessly and hopelessly in love, while the Duke remained carefree, only thinking of her as yet another woman to be pursued in search of amorous pleasure. She had lost her heart. She had no heart to lose. It had all gone badly and irrevocably wrong.

She turned for home. "What can I do now?" the words escaped her lips. If she stayed in London, it would mean further heartbreak not for the Duke but for herself. If she returned to the country that would mean the end of all her hopes. Either way she had nothing to expect from the Duke except the careless expression of his lust.

Perhaps . . . things will change . . . Perhaps his lust will change into love. She knew she was trying to deceive herself. All her actions had been aimed at deceiving the Duke, but instead they had duped her own heart. She had deceived her own heart. She was the author of her own unhappiness.

"Perhaps I can run away entirely, just disappear from the face of the earth." Lady Lancaster would like that. So perhaps would the Duke. He would be free of his boring wife in the country.

Would he miss the young girl who had caught his eye in London? A little, perhaps. But there would be other women to take his mind off the stranger on whom he had bestowed a careless kiss. There would be opera dancers and singers.

She just could not decide what to do. "I must talk to Emily," she thought. It was the measure of her own distress of mind. Usually it was Emily who asked advice of Clorinda. "I only wish Monsieur Lafayette had been in London still. He might have been able to help me."

Bravely she straightened up her slender form, and stepped out a little faster. The summer day had clouded slightly and it looked as if a shower was threatening. The occupants of the Park all seemed to be hurrying home to their work, or back to their place of business. It was time for her to be back too. She let herself quietly into the front door, and slipped upstairs. The walk in the Park had not been wasted. It had brought back some of her old resilience.

*   *   *

By the time Betty brought her the morning chocolate, she was pleased to see some color in the cheeks of her little Duchess. She had worried that she might find her pale and distressed. Instead, Clorinda was sitting up in bed with determined cheerfulness.

"I want you to pack up my things for me, Betty," she said. "Lay out my old traveling cloak, and also the dress I wore to arrive in London."

"Are we leaving so soon?" asked the astonished maid after a pause.

"It is high time I returned," said Clorinda with an assumption of good spirits. "I have enjoyed my time in London. I have bought a new wardrobe and learned about London society. There is nothing more for me to do here."

"But I thought, Your Grace . . ." The girl's voice trailed off. She was embarrassed for her mistress. She did not want to hurt her with further questions, and yet she wanted to know more.

"It was a silly idea, Betty," said Clorinda frankly. She managed to speak without a tremor. "I think it is time now that I returned to Westhampton, and made myself into a dutiful wife. After all I have had a fine holiday in London."

The maid looked disappointed with her answer for a while, but she soon forgot her preoccupation in brushing the wonderful red-gold hair and binding it with a green ribbon. "Your Grace looks lovely," she said warmly and comfortingly.

Downstairs Clorinda was amazed to discover that Lord Winterstoke had already arrived. He and Emily were making stilted conversation about the ball at Carlton House.

"I told Lord Winterstoke that I did not know when you would be down," said Emily in an embarrassed voice, "but he insisted on remaining."

"I am astonished to find His Lordship here so early," said Clorinda without any pleasure in her voice. Emily looked at her shrewdly.

"In pursuit of your charming company, it is no hardship to rise early," said Lord Winterstoke in a tone which Clorinda instantly recognized was one of gallantry mixed with an undercurrent of scarcely veiled threat.

Turning to Emily he went on rudely, "Madam, I wish to talk to Miss de Vere alone. She may or may not have confided in you about the events of last night. If not, I can assure you that it is necessary she should have some words in private with me."

Emily looked alarmed and confused. She knew nothing of this. "I have not told Mrs. Willoughby about last night," said Clorinda quietly. "I have not yet had time or opportunity to do so. But, Emily dear, Lord Winterstoke is right. I must have words with him privately. I know it is improper, but it is important."

"Very well," was all that Emily said. "I shall be next door in the green room, if you need me," she added significantly.

"Does your friend think that the ardor of my passion means instant rape?" asked Lord Winterstoke disagreeably as Emily left the room. "I am not so foolish, my dear, though were we still in the dark alleyways of Vauxhall Gardens I couldn't speak for my behavior. You are so lovely, you know."

"I am tired of your compliments," said Clorinda indignantly. "I have said I will see you, because you threatened me with exposure. Well, here I am. Is this not enough?"

"Let us not quarrel," said Lord Winterstoke smoothly. "I have a proposition to put to you." He paused.

"Last night I asked you if the Duke had deceived you by offering you marriage, and you said that you were not deceived. However, it is possible that you are still laboring under a misapprehension about the Duke. You are, after all, a newcomer to the fashionable world and it would be surprising therefore if you knew much about the Duke's background. He is, you will be interested to hear, already married."

Clorinda was silent. Taking her silence for astonishment, Lord Winterstoke continued. "I thought you did not know. Perhaps the Duke did not see fit to mention it.

"I understand he rarely talks either about his wife, or his marriage. But I have discovered that he entered into wedlock only recently with some countrified dowdy whom he has left in the country, where she belongs.

"She sounds exactly like the sort of woman that is totally unsuitable for Westhampton," he went on, his sarcastic voice warming to the task. "Ugly, stupid and a bore, I imagine. But there may be a scheme in his madness, after all.

"Most people who know about this ridiculous marriage of his think that it is Westhampton's way of protecting Lady Lancaster's reputation. His marriage should make it seem that he no longer cares for her.

"Then by leaving his boring wife in the country, he can enjoy the more spirited and sophisticated charms of Lady Lancaster in town. The gossips can be silenced by pointing to his marriage, and *he* can continue his affair."

He paused again. "Does all this come as a surprise to you?" he asked.

"I am interested, Lord Winterstoke," said Clorinda coldly, but truthfully. What he was saying— however upsetting—seemed only too plausible. But she did not want him to know just *how* interested she was. Still speaking icily she merely added, "Let us proceed. Fascinating though these details about the Duke's private life are, I still cannot see how they concern you."

"If the Duke cannot marry you, I nevertheless have a proposition for you, Miss de Vere," the leering Lord continued. "Come abroad with me instead. Forget the pompous Duke of Westhampton. His kisses are not the only ones that can thrill you.

"I swear I am as passionate and as skilled a lover as he. And, what is more to the point, I shall be far more generous. I will offer you any sum you may command. You see, Miss de Vere, I am as rich as the Duke and I want you. Oh yes, I want you far more than he."

His words made Clorinda shudder. She felt she must now say something. "Is this . . ." she managed, "is this a proposal of marriage, Lord Winterstoke?"

For a moment he looked embarrassed, then his natural self-confidence reasserted itself. "I consider I would shine more as a lover than a husband," he said. "But it might be marriage—later, if we are pleased with each other.

"Consider, Miss de Vere. You are a nobody. Your family and your fortune are completely unknown, though I have made extensive inquiries about both of them in the last few days.

"Cruel persons might class you as an adventuress. I do not. I admire your efforts to get into high society.

"I am only anxious that you should not waste your time with the Duke. You would find me so much better a bargain, my dear." A domineering smile was on his face.

Clorinda hardly knew what to say. She slowly began to realize that the man before her was not making an honest proposal of marriage. She assumed that this *must* be what he was talking about. But no. He was asking her . . . Clorinda de Villiers . . . to be his mistress . . . for money.

"If I understand you correctly," she said at last, "your proposition is neither flattering to my morals nor sympathetic to my aspirations. I think you had better leave this house, Lord Winterstoke."

"I shall go," he said, picking up his gloves and

169

cane. "But think hard, Miss de Vere, before you take such an outraged tone with me. I can tell the world that I saw you in the embrace of a married man."

"The Duke would kill you for that," said Clorinda fiercely. "He would call you out in a duel."

"I do not think so." Lord Winterstoke's sinister smile was broader than ever. "I shall not have to accept the challenge of a man who has duped high society."

"What do you mean?" Clorinda asked.

"What do you think, Miss de Vere? The members of his fashionable world can be very hard on people who have no proper family background. The Duke has brought you into fashion, Miss de Vere. What will his fashionable friends think when they discover that the girl he has danced with and been seen with is nothing more than a cheap adventuress.

"What will they say when I tell them that you have no family, and that nobody knows your background. And then when I tell them that you are the sort of girl who does not scruple to accept the amorous advances of a married man. He will be disgraced. He will be ruined."

"You would not be so cruel," she cried.

"No?" he laughed mockingly. "Come, Miss de Vere, I would do anything to win you. Think of my proposition. Name your terms. I shall be very generous I assure you. Weigh the advantages of what I can offer against the ruin that I shall otherwise bring to you. And to the Duke, too. I shall enjoy ruining him."

Clorinda stared at him dumbly. There seemed nothing she could do or say.

With a harsh chuckle Lord Winterstoke lifted her unresisting hand and took it to his hot lips, which lingered on it unpleasantly. Lifelessly the girl allowed the impertinent gesture. She did not know what to do.

But as he walked out of the door, closing it behind him, she listened to his footsteps walking out through the hall, and eventually through the front door. Then she shook the hand he had kissed with an expression of disgust, wringing it in the other hand, as if she could wash off the soiling kiss. It was thus that Emily, coming back into the room, found her sister.

"Oh, Emily," Clorinda could not help letting out a cry of anguish. She was not crying but she was painfully white. Her whole body was trembling, like an aspen tree in a storm.

"What did that awful Lord Winterstoke want?" asked Emily, catching her sister's hands in her own. "Oh, poor Clorinda."

"He wanted me . . . he wanted me . . . to become his mistress." The words were gasped in shaking tones. "Shocking isn't it, Emily?" she cried wildly. "But he threatened me, and I was frightened of what he might do."

The small hands in Emily's grasp shook with agitation, and Clorinda broke down in painful sobs. Her sister guided her to a settee, and sat down beside her. "Tell me all about it," she urged.

Between gasps for breath and pauses for further tears, Clorinda told all—how the Duke had led her off the ballroom to a small room away from the guests, how he had kissed her and how she had returned his kiss. Her voice was almost a whisper when she admitted it.

She told Emily everything that had followed—how the Duke had incomprehensibly suddenly thrust her away from him, how Lady Lancaster had arrived and made a scene, and finally how Lord Winterstoke had intervened, claiming to have seen it all.

"She told me that he was a rake," sobbed Clorinda, while Emily wisely did not ask who "he" was. She knew. "She said that he had seduced opera dancers and singers and," here a sob intervened, "a French woman."

"And did Lord Winterstoke hear all this?"

"No, he hadn't arrived then, but he was watching, he says. He says it is obvious that I am nothing but an adventuress trying to snare the Duke, for nobody knows anything about a de Vere family.

"He says he will disgrace me unless I consent to be his mistress, that he will tell everybody about finding me kissing the Duke. And he says the Duke will be ruined too for having foisted a nobody like me on the town. And that would mean that Robert and you would suffer too."

"Oh Clorinda," was all Emily could say for a moment. Then she asked: "What shall we do? I can hardly believe that a peer of the realm should be so base. Robert and Jack are next door. What shall I tell them? It is a shocking embroglio."

"Tell them the truth," Clorinda whispered. Then she spoke louder, swallowing her tears. "Tell them the plain truth about their sister. If they love me, they will understand."

As Emily rose to go next door to Jack and Robert, Clorinda wondered dully how she could continue to bear the agony she was experiencing. Lord Winterstoke's unvarnished proposal had come as a terrible shock. Did just the one kiss mean that he, and all men, would despise her? Was she utterly beyond the pale because of one reckless moment of passion?

It seemed the answer must be "yes." That one unwise kiss could ruin her in the eyes of the world —ay, and ruin the Duke, too.

The Duke would suffer, she reflected. His pride was so strong that he would surely feel all the pain of being brought low by a pretty piece of gossip. His whole family reputation would be at stake too.

She thought how distressed Mrs. Scotney, the housekeeper at Westhampton, would be to hear that her master had been in some trouble with a girl. Rumors about a mistress they would understand. Servants always knew everything, and a mistress or two was expected of men, it seemed. But rumors that the Duke had somehow deceived society would be something very different.

Now that she loved him, thought Clorinda, things had changed. A month ago she would have said that she cared nothing for the Westhampton family name, that it was nothing so old or so precious as the de Villiers name. But now it mattered to her as much as, nay more than, her own family. The Duke's pride she now understood. It was dear to her. She could not let him be harmed . . .

Jack burst in. "Just let me get my hands on Winterstoke," he shouted. "He'll not live to insult my sister. I shall call him out."

"I am not your sister, as far as he knows," said Clorinda dully. "I am just a Miss de Vere, remember? I am a person from nowhere, with no family that anybody knows of, no background and no fortune."

"I can call him out for insulting my sister Emily's guest," said Jack fiercely.

"Jack," said Clorinda quietly. "Neither you nor anybody will call out Lord Winterstoke. Don't you see that a duel would blacken my reputation forever? It would make an even bigger scandal. And it would ruin the Duke, too.

"Lord Winterstoke is a loathsome worm, but you must remember that he does not know who I am," she continued. "He only knows that I am a girl with apparently no family, and one who," here she swallowed her pride, "has been seen kissing a married man surreptitiously."

"She is right, you know, Jack." Robert broke in. "A duel will simply draw attention to all this. After all, we do not want it known that our sister has been offered a proposal more fit for a *fille de joie* than a decent young lady."

"But we must do something," fretted Jack. "Heavens, I shall barely be able to keep my hands off that cur, Winterstoke, when next I meet him."

"There is only one thing to do." Even as she said the words, Clorinda realized she had known all along what path she must take. She had not wanted to face that knowledge. "Miss de Vere will have to disappear forever. I shall become Clorinda de Villiers again, the quiet and dowdy wife in the country."

"Surely you will tell the Duke?" said Robert Willoughby. "Emily seems to think that perhaps he cares for you already."

"No, he doesn't care. Perhaps he would like to amuse himself with Miss de Vere, but that is all. For one thing he has never told Miss de Vere that he has a wife. Is that the action of a man who truly loves? Surely that deceit is just what one would expect from a rake? Besides," and her voice broke with the strain, "he pushed me away in disgust. He *rejected* me."

"But surely when he sees you again, he will recognize you now," said Robert.

"I do not think so. He will not see me as I am now. I shall go back to wearing my dowdy clothes, perhaps I shall even bleach my hair again. I shall continue in the deception. Who knows, he may learn to tolerate his country wife in the end. It may be that we can share some things together."

"But you will never tell him?" said Emily in dismay.

"I shall never tell him unless . . . unless I learn that he has truly loved Miss de Vere. But I do not think that is likely."

"Oh Clorinda, it seems so hard for you and I am so happy," Emily wept.

Clorinda found herself looking round their sad faces and searching for words of comfort. "It will cheer me to know that I have been helpful . . . After all the Duke has been generous to my family. Perhaps I shall persuade him to pay for you to get an Army commission, Jack. I should like it, if I could think that my marriage had helped you to give up gambling."

Despite his sympathy for her, Jack could not help reacting. His face lightened a little. But he said slowly, "I shall not let you down, Clorinda, any more. You have already done so much for me and Emily, that the least I can do in return is to stop gambling. I shall not place a bet again—I promise."

Jack's word was his bond. Clorinda knew that this was a heroic sacrifice. Although she felt altogether miserable, she managed a trembling smile at Jack. "You are a good brother," she said with all the conviction she could muster." I shall be comforted when I remember what you have said. It will make a difference to me when I am back in Westhampton."

"But in the meantime what are we going to do?" said Robert practically.

"I shall return to Westhampton as soon as possible. Jack will escort me, I dare say. I do not want to travel alone. His company will keep me . . ." she paused, "from being frightened. I am afraid Lord Winterstoke might try to pursue me, if he knew.

"But what about the rest of your lovely clothes?" asked Emily dismayed. "You were due for another fitting, and half of them have not yet been finished."

"I shall not need them in the country," replied her sister bleakly. "Besides I do not want any of them. I could not bear to wear them. Lady Lancaster said that the Duke had seduced a Frenchwoman. Who do you think she meant?"

"I have no idea," said Emily.

"Well, I have. Madame Latour told me that she knew the Duke. She told me that she had had an unhappy love affair. With an English aristocrat, she said. She also claimed that he had been an older man, but I think that was just to put me off the scent. I fear she may well be among the many women who have enjoyed more of my husband's love than I have."

"I can't believe that. Madame Latour is too old."

"She is not that old," argued Clorinda. "Anyway, I have my suspicions, and even if they are not true, it is enough to make me reluctant to wear her dresses. I do not need them anyway. All the world knows that the new Duchess of Westhampton is an ugly dowd. She must remain as ugly and dowdy as ever."

"Oh, Clorinda," moaned Emily. "Are you sure that you are doing the right thing. Shouldn't you confide in the Duke?"

"I would rather die." Clorinda turned toward the door, her figure erect, only the slightest tremor in her voice betraying her distress. "I shall go upstairs to see if Betty has finished packing. She must go on ahead by stagecoach."

As she went out of the room, Emily turned to Robert. "Can we let Clorinda leave like this?" she asked.

"I do not know," he said heavily. "I think we must let her decide for herself. We might do harm if we interfere. What else can be done anyway?"

"Should we not at least tell the Duke?" said Emily.

"I do not know that we can rely on his being understanding," replied Robert. "I do not know His Grace well, but it is said by everybody that he is as proud as Lucifer.

"What would he think of Clorinda's behavior? Would he not consider it wayward in the extreme? And would he take kindly to the deception we have practiced on him? I think she had best return to Westhampton. Jack, you must order a carriage."

Nodding his agreement, Jack left the room. It was obvious that he shared his sister's dismay but did not know what else to do. When he had gone, Robert Willoughby went on, "It is a mad scheme, Emily. Only my overwhelming love for you, and my gratitude to your sister, made me agree to it. We could never have succeeded."

Emily looked thoughtful. Unconsciously she placed her hand on Robert's. "Robert," she said, "I think that the trouble is not just Lord Winterstoke and his blackmailing threats. I think the trouble has to do with Clorinda's own feelings. I think she has fallen in love with the Duke. And, if she has, might not he have fallen in love with her?"

"I grant you that she attracts him. He would not have kissed her unless she did," said Robert. "But I think she is right in saying that he cannot be serious, if he has not revealed the truth about his marriage to her. Alas, I fear he is playing with her and that is all."

"But somehow I feel we should tell the Duke," said Emily persisting. "He does not look *unkind*, you know, Robert—a little formal, but not unkind. If we threw ourselves on his mercy without telling my sister . . ."

As if by magic, Clorinda's form appeared at the doorway. She was dressed simply and badly in the dress that she had worn for her journey to London. The same dowdy pelisse was on her shoulders. The new dark green pelisse with its swansdown trimming, the coquettish little bonnet and the little half boots had all been discarded. It was remarkable how different she looked without them. The beauty was still there—but it did not make itself noticed in the same way.

"You are not to tell the Duke behind my back, Emily," she said firmly. "If you do I shall never, never, never forgive you. I want your solemn word on it. And Robert's too. Promise me, both of you, that you will not tell the Duke anything about my real identity without my consent, whatever the circumstances."

They were silent, dismayed.

Clorinda spoke softly. "I did not think I would ever have to remind you, but I must. Both of you owe me this much," she said sadly.

"Oh Clorinda, of course, we promise." Emily flung herself into her sister's arms. "We know how much we are in your debt. You have sacrificed your happiness for ours. It's just that I thought the Duke might be able to cope with all this. I know that you are in love with him . . ."

"Don't." The word that broke from Clorinda's lip was one of pure pain. There was a silence. Everybody in the room realized that they were in the presence of grief.

She paused then added: "I have left my new clothes all packed up. I shall not be wanting them anymore. Perhaps you could find some way of disposing of them. All except the Eau de Nil gown. That one I am taking with me, as a reminder of my stay in London."

(9)

Rattling out of London by hired coach, Clorinda demanded the same promise from Jack that she had got from her sister and Robert Willoughby. "You have got to swear that you won't tell the Duke who I am," she said. "Now that I have disappeared he may ask you, but I must be able to rely on you to say nothing without my permission."

She was afraid that he, like Emily, would think the solution to her troubles was to tell everything to the Duke. It seemed as if her whole family had this touching faith that the Duke would solve their difficulties. She knew better. When she thought of telling the Duke, she could imagine the look of disgust his face would wear. "Do you swear it, Jack?" she repeated.

"All right, Clorinda, you have my word," was his reply.

She did not understand why, but she found herself worrying at the slowness of the hired coach horses. Compared with the Duke's grays, they were poor beasts able only to go at a moderate pace. She wished they might hurry more.

It was as if she had some kind of intuition that

told her delay would be fatal. She found herself looking anxiously out of the window calculating how long it would take to Westhampton, and trying to work out whether their coach could be overtaken by a pursuer. Lord Winterstoke? No, it was not he whom she had in mind. It was the figure of the Duke that obsessed and haunted her.

To take her mind off the thought, she said to Jack, "When did you become interested in the Army?"

"Oh, it was about three years ago," he replied. "When Wellington beat Napoleon at the Battle of Waterloo. I realized then what a glorious thing it must be to fight for your country. After that I started reading books about great generals and military history."

"Why didn't you tell us at Villiers Manor?"

"I knew there wasn't any point. Mama was already far from well. I knew she wouldn't like the thought of me becoming an officer. She would have worried about my safety. Besides there wasn't the money."

Clorinda nodded. For a moment she had forgotten that money was necessary. To become an officer, one had to buy the job by making a payment for it. It was an odd system, but one which was traditional in the British Army.

What a cursed thing money was, she thought. At every turn, it seemed to be necessary to have it. Obviously Jack had thought quite seriously about a military career. Here at last was something that held his interest, and would perhaps help him to stop being an irresponsible gambler. But, once again, it needed money.

Suddenly in the midst of these thoughts the coach ground to a creaking, swaying halt. "What the devil?" grumbled Jack, and jumped out to see what was going on. Clorinda stuck her head out of the window.

For a moment she thought they had been held up by a highwayman. There in the middle of the deserted road was a tall figure, dressed in black, holding a pistol. But it was no highwayman. It was the Duke, himself.

"Good day, Sir Jack de Villiers," drawled the familiar voice. Its languid tones had a cutting edge. "I find myself urgently anxious to talk to you. I believe I see Miss de Vere there in the coach."

"What the devil is that to you, Duke?" Jack's voice was full of bewilderment. Did the Duke know Clorinda's real identity, he wondered?

The next words from the Duke reassured him. "I would like to call you out here and now," said the figure with the gun through clenched teeth. "By God, I would run you through were I not your brother-in-law, de Villiers. But if I do, I shall only bring scandal upon Miss de Vere. I have therefore reserved a room at the White Hart just down the road a mile on, and I suggest we discuss this matter in privacy there."

"I have no option but to obey you while you point that pistol at me," said Jack in a sulky voice. He climbed back into the coach, and the curious entourage set off. The Duke had put away his pistol and was riding beside the carriage as if nothing untoward had occurred. Only the amazed expression of the postboy showed just how unusual the whole encounter had been.

Inside the vehicle, Jack whispered to his sister. "It's the Duke. He's insisting we stop. What do you think he wants?"

"I don't know," she replied. "Do you think he knows who I am?"

"No, he still thinks you're a Miss de Vere. He's furious about something, though. I can't make out what it could be."

At the White Hart a room had apparently been reserved, for the fat landlord came bustling out with many civil expressions about the honor done to his establishment by the Duke. Thinking he detected the light of curiosity in his eyes, Jack thought it best to say, "We are delighted that our good friend the Duke managed to catch up to us. The news he carries seemed urgent."

The landlord looked sceptical and Clorinda looked puzzled. As the door of the private parlor was shut behind them, she said to her brother, "What was all that about?"

"To put that rascally landlord off the scent, of course," said Jack. "I must say, Duke, that your dramatic intervention is damnably inconvenient. Now perhaps you will tell us what it is all about."

"Yes," chimed Clorinda. "You are seriously inconveniencing me and Jack. We want to continue our journey."

The Duke was grim-faced and stern. He faced the pair of them with an expression of barely-controlled fury. "Miss de Vere, you should be grateful to me. I have come to rescue you from your own imprudence. Marriage to Jack de Villiers would be foolish enough, but an elopment of this kind can only be madness . . ."

"An elopement?" echoed Clorinda in astonishment.

"Yes, an elopement. You know what I am talking about, de Villiers, even if Miss de Vere is innocent." The Duke's voice was harsh with rage. "I was about to call on you in London this morning, when I saw you setting out in a hired coach with Jack de Villiers. I determined to stop this nonsense."

Jack de Villiers had a smile on his lips. The funny side of what was happening had definitely struck him. "An elopement. That's rich," he could not help guffawing. He looked at his sister to see if she was going to share the joke, but she was as white as a sheet and did not look amused.

"I fail to see anything humorous in your behavior, de Villiers," the Duke was saying frigidly. "To persuade Miss de Vere into a runaway match is despicable. This sort of thing will create just the kind of scandal that could ruin her reputation forever."

"Well," said Jack, turning to Clorinda, "will you explain, or shall I?"

But his sister spoke in a voice that was as furious at the Duke's. "I will do nothing of the kind. I see no reason why the actions of Miss de Vere can concern the Duke of Westhampton. He has no rights over her."

Turning to the Duke she continued in biting tones. "You, Sir, seem to think you have the right to regulate my conduct. I do not know why. Your concern does not flatter me either. Is your persistent interference the result of a wager perhaps? Or is it designed to humiliate me?

"I am not one of your opera dancers or singers. Nor am I Lady Lancaster. The attentions of a mar-

185

ried man, such as yourself, can only be an insult to me. Even if they were honorable, they would still fill me with disgust. I find you and everything you stand for repulsive."

She stood panting with rage. The Duke had paled under the lash of her words. Just for a second she saw a flicker in his eye of something that might have been misery. But he controlled his emotion and his words were as coldly formal as ever. "I was not aware, Miss de Vere, that you found my attentions disgusting."

His reply infuriated her even further. Not content with deceiving her and behaving like a rake, now the man was trying to remind her of her shameful response to his kiss. She sought round for a way to hurt him. Womanlike, she wanted to wound back.

"You are too arrogant, Your Grace," she said with a semblance of his cold control. "I suppose a womanizer like yourself assumes that all women desire him. Well, I am an exception. I do not desire you at all. If you were the last man in the world, I would spurn you. Your riches and your title are not enough to tempt *me*. I have never met a man that I disliked so much. I hate you."

She did not know why the wounding words flowed so readily from her tongue. She did not pause for thought. She only knew that this man had hurt her pride as no man before him had done. Even the shameful suggestions of Lord Winterstoke had not hurt her with the same agony as the arrogance of the Duke of Westhampton had done. Was this love? She hated him with a passion as strong as death.

And yet something inside her yearned for an explanation, a reason, some justification for forgiving him. If only he would say that he loved her more than those other women. If only he would understand how humiliated she had been by his careless assumption of the right to judge her conduct.

The Duke's silence maddened her into further speech. "Lord Winterstoke has been kind enough to tell me that you are married, Your Grace. I found it slightly embarrassing to learn this fact from him, rather than from yourself. But perhaps you had some good reason for concealing this from me."

The Duke said nothing for a moment. Then in a dry precise voice, as if he had been ordering a glass of champagne at a ball, he said, "You will excuse me, I hope, Miss de Vere, if I order refreshments from the landlord. I hope you will grant me the opportunity of explaining my actions. I think I shall be able to persuade you of the honorable motives I had for intervening." Thus, he strode from the room.

"You will have to tell him," said Jack. His mirth had vanished at the scene he had witnessed. "You are an odd girl. Why did you want to bring up the fact that he's married? I don't understand why you are so upset about it. I thought it a great joke when he said we were eloping. Heavens, you must admit that it is extraordinarily like a bad play or a romance. Eloping with one's own sister!"

"I have no intention of telling him the truth," declared his sister, stamping one small foot with rage. Jack had never before seen her so angry. "I shall never forgive him for his arrogance. And you too, Jack. I shall never ever forgive you, if you break your oath."

"But we shall have to tell him something, Clorinda," objected her brother. "Dash it, we can't let him go on thinking we are eloping."

"You can tell him that you were taking me back to my home, Jack," said Clorinda reluctantly. "But mind you refuse to tell him where that is. I intend to continue my journey on my own, and I rely on you, Jack, to delay him sufficiently for me to make my escape."

"Clorinda, you can't do that." Jack found he was talking to an empty room. Clorinda had whisked out of it, slamming the door in a fury. "Little hell cat," he muttered. "She'll have to return when she finds that the horses have been unharnessed. Then perhaps she'll calm down a bit."

But Clorinda did not stop to enquire about the horses. She had no intention of proceeding in the same coach—a coach that the Duke would probably find only too easy to pursue.

Keeping a sharp look-out for him, she crept down the back stairs into the inn courtyard. There he was, chatting with the landlord just near the kitchen. The landlord was bowing and scraping. How obsequious they all are to him, she thought.

Turning, she ran out of the front door of the inn. She had no definite plan, but, being a resourceful girl, she felt sure something would turn up. There, indeed, in front of her was a stage coach just leaving.

Regardless of her dignity, she ran after it waving. The coachman looked around and obligingly stopped the lumbering vehicle. "Where are you going to, Miss?" he asked.

"As far as I can for a sovereign," said Clorinda, remembering almost too late that this, with some small change, was the sum total of her wealth.

"Climb aboard," he sang out cheerfully. She did so, squeezing herself in next to an apprentice. Two old clergymen and a skinny woman wearing an apron were sitting opposite.

After they had rumbled along for about a mile, she began to feel more secure. There was no sign of pursuit. Certainly Jack would not think of her catching a coach just at random. When she did not return he would assume she had hired some kind of vehicle, or even, perhaps, a horse.

Clorinda decided it would be prudent to discover the direction of the coach. Smiling politely at the clergymen, to the disapproval of the thin woman, she asked, "Where are we going?"

The clergymen looked amazed at this naive enquiry. "Do you not know where you are going to, young lady?" said the more elderly of them, who must have been about seventy.

"No, Sir," Clorinda admitted, "I was in haste to avoid a . . . the persecutions of a most disobliging gentleman, so I jumped in somewhat rashly. I have only a sovereign, so must discover how far that will take me."

"It will convey you, I think, as far as a hamlet that goes by the name of Little Repton," said the younger clergyman, who was a youthful sixty.

"Little Repton," mused Clorinda. The name sounded familiar but it took her two or three minutes to remember why. Then in a flash it came to her. Little Repton was the village where Monsieur Lafayette had his country retreat.

"That is marvelous," she said with enthusiasm. "Little Repton is just where I want to go. I have a good friend there who will help me."

"I hope that your good friend is somebody respectable, Miss," said the thin, acidulous woman disapprovingly.

"Oh, he's very respectable," said Clorinda sunnily. With Monsieur Lafayette, she would be safe, and—better still—he would advise her what to do. What a piece of luck it had been to get on a stage coach at random and then find it was going to take her to dear old Monsieur, who was just the person she needed in this contingency.

The journey to Little Repton was less tedious than she had expected. The passengers kept changing—the two clergymen alighting, and a farmer and some kind of small tradesmen taking their place. The thin woman, despite her unprepossessing looks, turned out to be good company and promised Clorindia to let her know when they were approaching her destination.

Little Repton turned out to be a small village, so small that it was almost a hamlet. Clorinda alighted with many expressions of good wishes from the thin woman, and looked around her with interest.

There were ten or twelve thatched cottages, a church, what looked to be the Manor farm, and a vicarage close to the church. It did not seem likely that Monsieur Lafayette would live in any of these. There was only one superior house otherwise.

It was not large enough to be a Manor house, but nevertheless it had a certain style. The windows were airy and set in stone. The approach at the front had a small but elegant drive. "This must be where Monsieur lives," thought Clorinda. "I only hope that he is at home."

A neatly dressed parlormaid answered the door for her. "Monsieur Lafayette is at home," she said in reply to Clorinda's query. "Who shall I tell him is calling?" Her good-natured face looked surprised at Clorinda's unexpected arrival on the doorstep. As well it might, thought Clorinda. She had neither luggage nor visible means of transport, the coach having continued on its way.

"Tell Monsieur that it is the Duchess of West-hampton," said Clorinda firmly.

At this the parlormaid looked frankly bewildered, but she nevertheless went to inform her master that a strange young lady calling herself a Duchess had arrived to see him. Clorinda heard a loud "Mon Dieu, my God," from Monsieur as he heard the name. The next moment he had bustled to the door, all solicitude.

"You are in trouble, my infant. I can see it in your face," he said promptly. "Mary bring this lady something to eat—claret and biscuits. Oh and bring a warm shawl for her too."

"Oh, I am so glad you were at home," sighed Clorinda, as she was led to the drawing room. Though it was nearly summer, a wood fire was burning on the hearth. The old gentleman sat her down upon a faded but comfortable chair. "I have so much to tell you," she said.

"Not now," he ordered, fussing round finding a footstool for her feet and a cushion for her back. Clorinda slightly wanted to laugh at his solicitude, but was too grateful for his kindness to let her affectionate amusement be shown.

The parlormaid returned with the wine and biscuits and two glasses. He poured one for Clorinda and one for himself. "Now you will sip that," he commanded and I will see you eat a biscuit before we speak of what you are doing here." He stood over her, while she did so. At first she found it difficult to swallow the dry biscuit, but after a few sips of wine, she managed.

"I did not know I was so tired," she said simply. A great feeling of relief and relaxation settled over her. "Thank you, Monsieur Lafayette. Where would I have been but for you?"

"Now," said the kind Frenchman, "it is time you told me all. You must confide in me utterly, if I am to give you good advice. For I imagine you are here for advice, not simply for the pleasure of seeing an old man such as myself."

Clorinda nodded. "I badly need your advice," she admitted.

"So what has been happening," he said. "I see from your face that much has occurred. I want the truth. The last time I saw you, you were preparing for the Prince Regent's ball, was it not? Now I find you alone, with no maid, no luggage and no companion. There is a lot for you to tell me."

Clorinda sighed again. The memory of their last meeting seemed aeons ago, a bright moment in a past that was now storm-clouded and threatening. Could it only have been a day ago? With an effort she wrenched her mind back to the magnificent ball in Carlton House, and began her narration. She told Monsieur everything. Once her elderly listener asked enlightenment.

"This kiss from the Duke?" he asked, "it repelled you?"

She blushed. "No, Monsieur," she confessed. "It did not . . . repel me." He did not persist for a further answer.

The only other remark he made during her tale, was when she told him about Lady Lancaster's outburst. "This mention of opera singers, this dancer in Vienna, and this Frenchwoman, you believed what Lady Lancaster told you?"

"Why not?" said Clorinda tiredly. "She is of the fashionable world, which I am not. Even my brother admits that it is known that the Duke has consorted with beautiful women all his life. It is only too likely to be true, I think. But perhaps you can guess what an awful suspicion crossed my mind when Lady Lancaster mentioned a Frenchwoman."

To her surprise the old man said nothing, but "Continue." She had thought he would immediately perceive that she worried lest Madame Latour was the French woman referred to by Lady Lancaster. She had thought he would instantly defend his friend to her.

She obeyed his command to continue with her tale. He listened to all the rest of it, including the Duke's sudden appearance on the road, and her arrival at Little Repton. Occasionally he rapped his gnarled but elegant long fingers against the side of his chair. She could not tell from his expression what he was thinking.

"That is all," she said with a sigh, when she had explained the last part of her story. "I came here for I had nowhere else to go. I could not bear to let my brother tell the Duke who I was. It was just too horrible—the thought of confessing to him and seeing his disgust. I could not face it."

Monsieur Lafeyette said nothing about her tale at first. His first words were entirely practical. "We must ensure that your brother and sister know that you are safe," he said. "I will send my groom with a letter now, and your sister will receive it by this evening."

Walking across the room, he opened a walnut-veneered desk and placed upon it a delicately scented piece of paper and a quill pen. Seated at the desk,

Clorinda wrote to Emily saying she had taken refuge with Monsieur Lafayette, and she was well and that she would be returning to Westhampton the following day. "I earnestly implore you, dearest sister, to hold Robert and Jack to their oath and not to reveal that Miss de Vere and the Duchess of Westhampton are one and the same person. Try if you can, to restrain our brother from recklessly calling out Lord Winterstoke." She wanted to add "or the Duke" but somehow she could not bring herself to go into the details of that scene in the White Hart from which she had fled.

When she had finished it, the old man called in the parlormaid and gave her instructions to send the groom to London with the note.

"Now to the real business," said he, seating himself back in the chair by the fire. "Now you shall tell me not what has happened, but what you feel about it. Lord Winterstoke, for instance. Do you hate this man?"

"Hate *him?*" Clorinda could not help smiling. "No, he is an odious worm but he is of no importance, save for his malice. I am afraid of what he may do to harm the Duke. But I do not hate him. It is the Duke that I hate. I have never before felt such a great deal of hatred toward one man." Her eyes flashed.

"It is an odd thing that you should hate him so strongly," said Monsieur Lafayette with a quizzical expression she could not understand. "Hating a husband is not a good beginning to married life, I think."

"My whole marriage is a mockery," said Clorinda bitterly. "In London I thought I had fallen in love with the Duke, but then when he stopped our coach so arrogantly, I knew it was not love. I hate him."

"Yet you would flee London to save his reputation?" persisted the fatherly figure by her side.

"I suppose so." Clorinda's reaction was one of anguish. "I do not understand. It is all such a muddle," she said childishly. "It is as if I loved him with my whole being and hated him at the same time. I have never before experienced such a tangle of feelings, Monsieur. I had hoped you might help me cope with it."

"Love is a great deceiver," said the old man slowly. "That is why for centuries men have called Cupid blind. It is not easy, if we love—or if we hate—to know the reasons why."

Then, with a change of conversation he said, "Perhaps you will help me pick some of my roses in the garden. I am an old man and I should value your company. I will hold the basket while you pluck the blooms."

"Perhaps his mind wanders a bit with his age," thought Clorinda as she followed him out of the room in search of a wicker basket for the flowers. She did not like to object to this employment, since he had been so kind to her. But she was impatient. She had come for advice, and all he seemed to do was to suggest that she pick roses!

Behind the house was a walled garden that caught the sun. There was every kind of simple cottage flower. Marigolds, candy tufts, Lad's love, periwinkle, stocks, gilliflowers and sweet-smelling thyme in clumps everywhere. Bees and butterflies went to and fro across the blooms, filling the air with their color and humming sound.

But it was the roses that were spectacular. There was a kind of alleyway in which great banks of roses had been encouraged to grow up on either side, rambling as they wished over wooden supports, so that either side was a mass of blooms. The petals had tumbled to the ground from the overblown roses, so that it was like walking on a carpet of flowers.

"These are Gloire de Dijon roses," said her host, handing her a pair of sharp cutters. "There was such an alleyway, only larger, at our family's chateau, before the Terror."

Clorinda began to cut the stems of the roses. It was more difficult than she had thought. Although the blossoms were of surpassing color and scent, there were many cruel thorns among them. By the time she had gathered enough for a large bowlful she had torn her white fingers several times upon the thorns. Out of politeness she did not mention this to her companion.

When they returned to the house, Monsieur Lafayette gave the basket of flowers to the maid to be put into a vase. "Thank you, my dear, for your aid," he said. "I fear that you have wounded yourself in picking the flowers."

"It is nothing," said the girl politely. "But the thorns were unusually sharp. I have never known such marvelous flowers. What a pity they have such thorns!"

"My dear," said the old man. "My invitation to pick roses was not just the whim of an aging Frenchman. There is a lesson from flowers, if we will learn it. You are right. Those roses are some of the finest in blossom and scent to be found in Europe. And likewise their thorns are the sharpest. It is as if the beauty of the blossoms cannot be got without the pain of the thorns."

"Are you trying to tell me, Monsieur Lafayette,

that this is the same with love?" said Clorinda quickly.

"It is not just I who say this. All the great poets have shared the same thought. Those who would pluck the flowers of love must be prepared to brave the thorns. There is no room for the faint-hearted who wish for the joys without the pains, Clorinda.

"That is why I say you must go back to Westhampton. You cannot stay there in retreat from the battle of life. Not if you want the chance of finding out your true love.

"I have three things of importance to tell you, my child," he went on. "The first is to tell you about the woman I loved, for your destiny is bound up with her story. She is dead now, but sometimes I think she is still close to me. She was so very beautiful . . ." He paused. Clorinda remained silent. It was as if his eyes were focused far, far away and could see all that beauty before them.

"She was the Duchess of Westhampton," he said slowly.

Clorinda stifled a gasp of surprise. It was the Duke's mother of whom they talked, that lively though sad lady whose portrait hung in the Westhampton library. "Then you must be . . . you must be," she began.

"I am the Marquis de Rochefoucauld de la Lafayette," said the old man proudly. The ancient French title slipped with ease from his lips. "But I have forgone my title, my dear. That is all part of the past that is almost too painful to remember. But as you say I am the Marquis who ran off with the Duchess.

"Why did you do this?" Clorinda whispered the question. At last she would find out the truth.

197

"It was more than thirty years ago. The Duchess was unhappy with her husband. The sixth Duke was a harsh man, and a rake. His mistresses were the byword of London. He was incapable of being discreet about it.

"When I met the Duchess I fell instantly in love. I was a young man then, my dear, and I was foolish. I implored her to leave her husband, to come away with me. And she consented, perhaps out of love, perhaps out of despair. I do not know."

"But what happened to her. How did she die?" asked Clorinda.

"She died in childbirth. Her daughter died with her." The old man's voice held a note of such pain that Clorinda could hardly bear it. Then he seemed to rouse himself. "I am telling you this because I believe it may help you.

"You see there was one person who suffered more than I did—the Duchess's son. He lost his mother, for she could not take him with us. His father was not an affectionate man. I do not think it can have been easy for the little boy.

"That was how we wronged him, Marie and I. I did not realize how deeply, but I think she did. She was never truly happy with me. I think the feeling of that wrong stayed with her. And I . . . now I too realize that it was not right for us to snatch at happiness at the expense of a child."

"Is that why you are helping me?" said Clorinda shyly.

"It is partly why, but also because I do not wish to see you suffer as I have suffered."

"There is a difference, Monsieur le Marquis," said Clorinda. "You see, I do not think that the Duke loves me."

He smiled gently and patted her hand. "Are you sure? You must find out, you know? You must not despair too early."

"I must find out," she echoed obediently. As she said the words it was as if a piece of the jigsaw slipped into place. She had told Emily and Robert and Jack earlier that day that Miss de Vere must disappear and that the dowdy Duchess would take her place—forever.

Suddenly she realized there was another way. She *would* go back and become the dowdy Duchess again. But she would use her disguise to find out the truth about the Duke's heart. She would tax him with his behavior in London, and ask him about Miss de Vere. If he told her that it had simply been a flirtation, well, she would remain the countrified wife he thought her. But if . . . if he said he had fallen in love with Miss de Vere, then she could reveal her true identity. Suddenly she knew this was what she must do.

The Frenchman was still talking, "And now there is something more I must tell you. It is about Madame Genevieve Latour this time. It is a day for confessions, my infant.

"You tell me that you are suspicious lest she has been the mistress of the Duke of Westhampton. Well, your suspicions are well founded."

"So it was all a plot by her." Clorinda was horrified by this disclosure.

"Softly, little one," he answered. "Her lover was not this Duke. It was his father.

"She knows your Duke, as she has told you. But she knows him as a benefactor not a lover. It was he who helped her after his father abandoned her and died. The present Duke was a young man but he had a sense of justice and he felt that something must be done to put right the wrong of his father. That is why he gave her the money, which she used to start her dressmaking business."

"I had thought perhaps . . ."

"I know, little one. But your suspicions were ill founded. Remember that Lady Lancaster's words were designed to wound."

"But what about the opera dancers she spoke of? And the singer in Vienna?" asked Clorinda.

"This is the third and last thing that I must tell you, infant. Men are not as women are and it is foolish to pretend that they are. Men are different."

"Mama used to say that too," said Clorinda, her mind going back to those far off secure days in Villiers Manor.

"Your Mama was a wise woman," said the old man by her side. "When women love, it is a thing for life, a thing so important that they do not love easily. Nor do they stop loving even when hope is gone."

He paused, then went on. "But there is a kind of love that men can feel. Perhaps I should say that men can give their bodies without giving their hearts. For them dalliance is a matter of little importance.

"It may be true that your Duke has enjoyed a brief liaison with an opera dancer or a singer, just as he has enjoyed one with Lady Lancaster. But if the Duke has had agreeable affairs with women, it does not mean he had no heart. If he loves truly and deeply then these affairs will be nothing but the indiscretions of the past.

"My dear, the woman whom he loves must welcome him as he is. She must not punish him for those past follies. She must forget them for his sake, not

200

looking back ever, but looking forward to the happiness which such a love will undoubtedly bring.

"Your Duke has had an upbringing without the love of a mother, and without, I should guess, much love from his father. You cannot expect him to understand his maladroit behavior."

At this well-timed moment the parlormaid came in to announce that a meal was served. As they moved out of the drawing room into the paneled old dining chamber, Clorinda noticed how beautifully the house was kept. Every piece of furniture shimmered with beeswax polish. And a faint odor of roses seemed to hover in the air.

The meal in front of them was very simple. It could not have been more different from the rich viands and subtle sauces that were served at Westhampton, thought Clorinda.

Yet she enjoyed it enormously—fresh crusty cottage bread, warm nourishing chicken soup, and thick slices of country cheese. She discovered that she had quite an appetite.

Monsieur Lafayette—she could not call him the Marquis since he had said the title was part of a past he did not want to recall—talked about books. She had read widely, and discovered that she could hold her own in a literary conversation. He discussed French literature, and then told her a little about the many interesting scenes he had witnessed in his youth, in the days before the French Revolution destroyed aristocratic life.

The same quiet atmosphere persisted when, after supper, they repaired to the drawing room. Clorinda, at his request, played him some simple ballads on the piano, accompanying her singing. She did not have a trained voice, but it was sweet and tuneful and so pure in tone that it might almost have been the voice of a young choirboy.

A bed chamber had been prepared for her. The bowl of roses she had picked adorned an old-fashioned chest of drawers, and gave its scent out to everything in the room. A faint smell of spices came from the lower drawer, where Clorinda discovered cloves and dried bags of Lad's love had been placed to keep the moths away from the household linen.

By the bed she noticed a small leather volume of some of Shakespeare's more famous speeches. "I wonder if it includes my favorite," she thought, and turned the leaves till she discovered the passage, "To be, or not to be." Slowly she read it. "I shall take arms against my sea of troubles," she told herself, as she slipped between the cool sheets faintly smelling of the garden where they had been aired. "I shall take arms, and I shall conquer."

(10)

The garden at Westhampton was the neatest and most formal one Clorinda had ever seen. An earlier Duke had obviously spent time at the court of Versailles, for the grounds were laid out in the formal French style of a previous age.

As Clorinda strolled round its neat gravel paths and flower beds edged with little box hedges, wave after wave of fragrance eddied into the air about her. It was rather like being bathed in different perfumes—one after another, according to which flowers graced the beds.

She was picking flowers in a rather desultory fashion. There did not seem very much else to do that day. It was very quiet at the big house, and very peaceful with the Duke away.

She had arrived two days before to find an enthusiastic welcome from the household staff. Monsieur Lafayette had arranged for her to travel back by the Duke's traveling coach. Nobody seemed to know when the Duke was expected back, but everything was in readiness in case he should take a whim to return. It was just as he had said that second day of their marriage—his household was trained to expect him at any time.

To Clorinda's surprise nobody, not even Mrs. Scotney, the housekeeper, had their suspicions of what she had been doing. Mrs. Scotney, it is true, had asked about her sister's health—but otherwise showed little interest in the matter. It was as if the world outside Westhampton hardly existed for them.

Clorinda had gone back to her role as the dowdy Duchess. She wore hats whenever possible, and little caps to hide the glorious hair. That afternoon, she was dressed in one of the unfashionable day dresses that the village dressmaker had run up. A sunbonnet in straw crammed down low over her head hid the red-gold curls, and shaded the deep green eyes from view.

She had brought a root of the Gloire de Dijon rose from Monsieur Lafayette's garden. "I hope it will bloom for you as it bloomed for me," said the old man with touching concern. "I feel somehow it will. I am perhaps a little clairvoyant in these things my dear, and though I see storms and an overcast sky for you now, I can see a rainbow at the end of it."

Inspired by his words, she had determined that she must start doing her duty as a Duchess. There were many goodwill tasks that she would be expected to perform. The day before she had called upon the vicar to ask which families were in need of help from the Hall, and she had been heartened by his obvious pleasure.

It was all part of her decision to stop leading a selfish life. Before, when she had gone to London, she had been avid for a chance to enjoy the fashionable life. She had considered that the wordly routine of dancing, and parties and gossip was the highest to which any woman might aspire. She had wanted to become one of the stars in that glittering social whirl.

Now she knew better. She knew that heartbreak could too often underlie the shimmer of the rich salons; that immortality and vice, which looked attractive in fine clothes and polished manners, were just as ugly in town as in the country. Lord Winterstoke had been proof of that.

One good thing, indeed, had arisen from that immoral peer's disgraceful behavior, she thought. On her arrival at Westhampton there had been a hasty letter from Jack.

In it, he had repeated his promise that from now on he would avoid gambling. "My eyes are now open to Winterstoke and his Set," read the scrawling hand. "Nothing would induce me to have any connection with them again, dear Sister."

He had kept his word not to tell the Duke of Clorinda's identity. "There was a fine set-to when you disappeared," he wrote, "with the Duke challenging me to a duel, and the devil of it there was I refusing to fight.

"It was behavior I had not thought possible, and indeed it would have shamed me had people discovered it. I said that as his Brother-in-Law it ill became me to brawl with him. I had thought for a moment that the Duke would land me a blow in the face for that, but then he becomes very silent, whether thinking of his Miss de Vere or his Duchess I leave to you to determine, dear Sister.

"I dare swear that the man is in Torment," finished the letter cheerily. "I could find it in my heart to pity Westhampton. He was in despair at your loss and has sent servants to every inn in the county. He would call out the Bow Street runners, I think, but that I have told him it will cause rather than cure Scandal."

Clorinda could not help smiling at the letter. Jack had never been one to write letters at all, and this must have taken a heroic effort from him. "Dear Brother," she had written back hurriedly, "there is neither Time nor Opportunity for an explanation, but I assure you I will end the Deception soon either by telling the Duke all, or by burying Miss de Vere in Oblivion forever."

She was still musing at the change in her brother, when she heard the sound of galloping hooves upon the road up to the Hall. The speed at which they approached, and the almost magical abruptness of their halt in front of the Hall, could only denote the Duke's grays. No other pair could have been so well in hand, driven so fast and stopped so exactly.

Hurriedly she snatched up an armful of the flowers, and held them close to her so that her face was shaded by them, as well as the sunbonnet. Nothing could be seen of her eyes now.

The tall figure of the Duke was coming across the lawn toward the flower beds. He was more carelessly dressed than she had ever thought possible. The arts of the dandy that had characterized his elaborate cravats were now all forgotten. Instead of its snowwhite folds, he wore just a neckerchief loosely knotted. His boots were travel worn and stained.

His face looked careworn and, Clorinda had to admit, unhappy. The aquiline nose and frowning brows were etched into his face, but the arrogance that usually marked his expression was missing, In its place was—there was no other word for it—misery.

But his manners were as polished as ever. "Your servant, Madam." His bow was faultless. Clorinda realized that the man had steeled himself to show no signs of his inner wounds. She merely inclined her head in reply to the bow.

"Madam Duchess, there is a matter of some import that I must discuss with you in private," said the Duke harshly. He took the basket from her and offered her his arm. Then he led her to a small stone bench at the end of the garden, where the warm stone wall supported rambling roses and moss roses of the sort an earlier generation must have loved.

When she was seated, he did not join her. Instead he lounged uneasily in front of her. For a moment Clorinda was reminded of a small unhappy boy owning up to some fault. "Madam," the Duke said, "what I have to say will probably upset you. It must be said, though. I want a divorce."

"A divorce?" Clorinda echoed the words in amazement. She had certainly never envisaged this. For a moment she was nonplussed.

"Oh, I know how badly I am behaving," the Duke went on. "It is a shameful demand to make to a lady who has done me no harm. There is nothing in *your* behavior . . . in our marriage . . . that is wrong. It is simply that it is not a proper marriage. We married for reasons of convenience, my convenience, I own it. But there was . . . and can be . . . no love."

"Love, your grace?" Clorinda had decided to test him further. "When your generous proposal reached me at Villiers Manor, love did not seem to be required of me, or indeed offered by you. We had, as I am sure you recollect, never met, and you showed no eagerness to do so before the wedding ceremony. I find this talk of love strange coming from you."

"You are justified in everything you say. I bitterly regret my past behavior," said the Duke. "When I offered you my hand, it is true that I did not think love necessary. Indeed I did not wish love to be part of the bargain. Then I considered love the invention of want-wit poets and wayward women. But now I know that love is necessary. I have discovered what love really is."

"And what is it?" said Clorinda sharply, trying to make her voice as unlike Miss de Vere's had been as possible. "Are you talking about some love affair, Your Grace. Is there trouble with an arrangement that is not proceeding smoothly? Is this your love?"

The Duke groaned. "I was afraid you might think that was all. I know my reputation . . . involves a certain type of woman. I have asked for these reproaches.

"What can I say? I freely own that I too would have thought that was the reality of love—an amusing affair, the pleasures of a man of the world. Once I would have thought that, now I know differently."

"You mean that you are no longer interested in opera dancers, singers . . . in Lady Lancaster." Clorinda probed relentlessly.

"My dear," said the Duke, and his voice was full of a kind of paternal weariness. "You have lived so retired in the country that you do not understand there was no harm in these little amusements—well, very little harm. None of the ladies whose affections I engaged had a heart to be broken. It was a series of transactions. My money in return for their bodies. I have never trifled with the young and innocent."

"Never?"

"My God, what can I say?" the Duke cried out. "It is true that up to now I have never had dealings with innocence. But now," he passed a hand over his brow with a gesture of despair, "now I have fallen in love with . . . a schoolroom Miss, and it is all chaos to me."

"She will no doubt not remain innocent for long," said Clorinda spitefully. "I suppose she will become like Lady Lancaster."

For a second she thought that he was going to strike her. "You will never again make such a suggestion," he hissed through clenched teeth. "The girl I love is too pure, too divinely innocent, to be mentioned in the same breath as women like Lady Lancaster."

"What sort of girl is she?" asked Clorinda disdainfully.

"She is beautiful, of course, yet not beautiful in the way of ordinary beauties," said the Duke. His eyes softened and fixed their gaze at the rambler roses, as if lingering over a memory. His voice was quiet and gentle. "She has green, green eyes, hair like red-gold, and an odd elfin face. She is graceful and when she waltzes it is like dancing on air. When she is angry, her eyes seem to grow huge and they flash and glitter."

Clorinda could hardly believe that he could be so close and not recognize her. She shrunk into the badly made dress, and kept her eyes on the gravel at her feet. She drank in the words like nectar, avid for whatever he was going to say next.

The paean of praise continued "When I first met her, I thought perhaps she was some fille de joie. Then I realized that her freedom and her spirit came from innocence, not from worldliness. I do not know her family, but I know she is gently bred. I imagine her blood is as blue as my own, though I freely confess I do not care a jot. I should not care if she were a scullion's daughter . . ."

Clorinda broke in on his rhapsody. She was finding it difficult to conceal her own emotion. "Your Grace," she said in a voice she hoped was formal and cold, "none of this explains why you are seeking a divorce. I cannot understand why you should be telling me, your wife, about this . . . female you have met.

"It seems to me that you face two possibilities. You can forget this unknown girl, or you can make her your mistress. For my part, I believe this is just a passing fancy. I am willing to pretend that we have never discussed the matter."

With that she rose from the bench, taking the basket from the Duke's unresisting hands. She walked firmly back to the Hall. He did not try to follow her. It was as if he was stunned by her reaction.

Instead, he sank onto the bench she had quitted, gazing at the clusters of old-fashioned blooms rambling down the wall. Just before she entered the Hall, she noticed him bending down to smell one of the blooms. She wondered if the scent of the real roses perhaps reminded him of the odor of rosewater. She could hear his voice now, at Vauxhall Gardens, saying to her "you smell of rosewater. How old are you?"

Now he was suffering, she knew. All her old antagonism vanished, as she thought of his unhappiness—just as his own arrogance had suddenly deserted him. Her heart sung a nameless melody of happiness as she trod the stairs up to her bedroom.

The faithful Betty was waiting for her, agog with excitement. The girl either knew, or sensed, that this was an evening which would mean everything to her mistress. Without instructions, she had already laid out ready the Eau de Nil dress. On the dressing table was the rosewater, and the brush to make the red curls glow.

Laid gently on the bed, the greenish dress still looked marvelous. In the daunting formality of Westhampton, it nevertheless kept all its old mystery. Its glinting soft material, indeed, seemed to have taken on a new dignity. It flickered and shone in the candlelight from the lustres on the wall. The pale green dissolved into a mixture of darting yellow, orange and golden fire.

"Can I brush your hair out, Your Grace?" asked Betty softly, as Clorinda took her seat at the dressing table.

"Please do." Freed from the unbecoming straw sunbonnet, the red-gold strands shone and twinkled as the brush ran through them. They sprang back to life, glowing with vivid color. While Betty brushed and brushed a hundred strokes, Clorinda took a long look at herself in the mirror.

It was amazing, she thought, how the dowdy Duchess could be transformed in a twinkling of an eye into the glamorous Miss de Vere. With a slight wrap about her shoulders and her hair swinging loose she was now the elfin beauty that the Duke so adored.

She shivered, whether from anticipation or fear she could not tell. "Do not wait up for me, Betty," was all that she said. The girl knew what she meant. She put down the brush and helped her mistress with the frock, placing it so gently over her head so not a lock of hair was disarranged.

With a quiver of anxiety, Clorinda wondered what he would say when he discovered that she, his dowdy countrified wife, was the Miss de Vere he so much loved. Would he be furious? Disgusted at what might be thought a vulgar prank? It was a gamble, she realized, a gamble that perhaps even Jack in his most dissipated days might have thought twice before accepting. For this was bigger than any wager he had ever made. On the outcome hung her whole life's happiness. She was taking a chance with love.

Slowly she walked down the stairs. There was no sign of the Duke.

There were questions that remained unanswered, questions she would like to ask him—perhaps this was the time. Lady Lancaster was one of these questions. Had the Duke decided he no longer cared for her? What would happen to her?

She gave her instructions to the butler to tell the Duke that she would await him in the library before dinner. He would surely come.

As she waited in the reassuring company of the leatherbound volumes, she thought suddenly of Villiers Manor, her childhood home. It seemed remote, unattainable, something belonging to the far off past.

"This is my home now," she thought, and the idea caught her unawares. The love she now felt for

Westhampton had grown up without her knowledge. She loved not only the house, but the servants in it —faithful Betty, conscientious Mrs. Scotney, and the minor servants. She realized that she would be severely unhappy if she had to leave.

For comfort she looked up at the picture of the last Duchess. If only Monsieur Lafayette could have seen the picture. But perhaps he had a better likeness in his memory. The smiling woman, a hint of tragedy behind the smile, looked down on her. The virgin bride and the erring wife were very close to each other, joined in their desire for true love.

Clorinda took up her position near the window. The heavy curtain not yet drawn protected her from the full light of the candles in the lustres on the wall. Through the glass slanted shafts of rose-red light from the last dying embers of the setting sun.

When the Duke entered, he could see only her slim body outlined against the light. Her face was turned from him, looking out through the window toward the deer park.

He scarcely glanced at her. He was evidently more concerned with his own thoughts than her physical presence. Pacing up and down the room, he said urgently, "I must ask again for a divorce. It is the only way. God knows I have racked my brains day and night, but I can see no other way than this."

"But I do not want to divorce you," said Clorinda truthfully, still gazing out of the window. "I do not understand this change of heart you seem to have had."

"Unless you believe in love, the possibility of a true and perfect love, you will not ever be able to understand. To me this marriage of ours is a sin against that love."

"Does she know?"

Her abrupt question caught him unawares. "Does she know what?" he asked in a bewildered tone.

"This female you love," explained Clorinda, "does she know that your love for her means the ruin of our marriage? Does she know that thanks to her, you are now trying to persuade me to accept the shame of a divorce?"

"She does not," the words were wrenched from him. "I have been such a blind, mad fool. I treated her as if she was . . . like the other women. Then to crown my folly I did not tell her I was already married. Instead she discovered that from other people."

"You deceived her." Clorinda's voice was pitiless.

"Not intentionally." His voice rang out with anguish. "I meant to tell her. But somehow I could not find the words or the occasion. She was so pure . . . so innocent . . ."

"And where is she now?"

"I have lost her. I thought she was eloping with . . . with an unsuitable young man, and like an idiot I pursued them both. I had no right to intervene, but I was anxious to save her from her folly."

Clorinda had to hide a smile. How typical of a man. Even now he was protecting her brother, Jack, from his sister's wrath. The Duke would never tell tales, it seemed.

He was continuing his self-accusation. "I was mad with jealousy and she fled from me. I have hunted through the whole of the county, asked questions of every toll keeper from London to Brighton, bribed inn servants, bullied ostlers. I have not rested night and day, since that frightful moment when I found she had gone."

"And you still ask me for a divorce. Even though you do not know where the girl is? What is this wilful obsession, Your Grace?"

"It is not an obsession." The Duke spoke tiredly. "I love her. I do not know if she loves me, but the only reparation I can make for my behavior toward her is to free myself from this marriage . . . and wait . . . and hope."

He was utterly humbled now.

"You need not wait long." With these low words, so soft that they could scarcely be heard, Clorinda turned from the window and faced the Duke. She took a step forward into a pool of light thrown by a heavy silver candelabra.

The Duke looked at her. He stood perfectly still and perfectly silent, as if he could not believe the evidence of his own eyes. The light shone on her red-gold hair, and danced among the green folds of her silk dress, echoing the green of her huge eyes.

Clorinda looked utterly serious. Then a shy little smile crept over her face. "Here is the girl you are seeking," she said, and her voice trembled with emotion. She took two more steps forward, shyly and delicately, like a young fawn stepping out of the forest for the first time.

Still the Duke was dumb. His first words were somber. "Now I know I am in truth mad," he said conversationally as if addressing himself. "This must be an illusion."

"It is no illusion. I am the Duchess of Westhampton, the Clorinda de Villiers you wed, and whom you left here in the country. But I am also the Miss de Vere you rescued that night at Vauxhall Gardens. You danced with me at Carlton House." Her voice dropped again. "You . . . kissed me there."

With one giant stride he was at her feet, kneeling there looking up at her. To see the arrogant Duke brought so low, should have been sweet revenge for Clorinda. But it gave her no pleasure.

Flushing with shame for him, she tried to raise him. "No, no," he cried. "Can you forgive me? I have been so blind that I could not even see my heart's desire."

"Please get up . . . Julian." Clorinda blushed as she used his first name. He rose to his feet.

It was just in time. A warning cough at the door betrayed the presence of the butler. Clorinda's blush deepened, but the Duke raised his eyebrows as if nothing had happened. "What is it?" he said haughtily, but a faint tinge of pink along his sculptured cheek bones showed his embarrassment.

"Dinner is served, Your Grace," was the correct and colorless reply.

The butler was too good a servant to exhibit his amazement at the sight of the Duke, rising from what seemed to have been a kneeling position. Later on he would preserve his discretion in the servant's hall, keeping his secret from his inferiors. Perhaps in the housekeeper's room he might hint . . . just hint, to Mrs. Scotney of what he had seen . . .

*   *   *

If the Duke's conversation was a little absent-minded, and if the Duchess showed a distressing tendency to ignore what was being served to her, the footmen did not notice. As the many varied courses

216

with the usual subtle sauces succeeded one another, it looked to the outsiders as if a married couple were having a normal quiet evening together.

"How is Jack? Did you find him well?" asked Clorinda politely from her end of the mahogany table.

"Your brother would have sent his regards, I dare say, had he known what we would be dining *like this* together," said the Duke with equal politeness. Only a twinkle in his eye and a softening of his gaze as it rested on the slim young girl at the other end of the long table, betrayed his warmth.

"In the circumstances, Jack remained discreet," he went on. "I have to confess that I was rather severe on him. Only his relationship to you spared him something worse than harsh words."

"I believe he recently refused to fight a duel," said Clorinda naughtily. Fortunately, she thought, the servants will never realize what this all means.

"That is true," said the Duke. "Devilish angry with him I was too. It must have been difficult for him. I appreciate his dilemma now. At the time I did not. He told me about Winterstoke, you know?"

Clorinda blushed slightly. Though the servants could not understand the meaning, nevertheless the introduction of Lord Winterstoke's name caused her a moment of panic. "I am glad," she spoke with an effort, searching for a way that would not reveal too much.

"Lord Winterstoke was the reason that I left my sister in such haste," she went on. "He was . . . very pressing about a certain matter.

"There is one good thing—Jack will have less to do with him now. And he has promised to give up his gambling," said Clorinda turning the talk into less dangerous channels. Then a thought struck her. "There is something I want to ask you—a favor. It is for Jack. I have promised to beg you to give him a commission in the Army."

"What a good idea," said the Duke and the conversation proceeded.

Back in the blue salon, after the interminable meal was over, he ordered the butler to leave the cognac bottle for himself, and a glass of ratafia for Clorinda.

Pouring himself a glass, he said in an old tone. "I think that I once said the de Villiers come expensive. I fear you are a mercenary wife, Duchess. First you marry me so you can pay off your wretched brother's debts. Now you want me to buy him a commission."

Clorinda's face paled. "It is not true," she gasped. "I know I was mercenary when I married you, but I am not now. I . . . love you."

The Duke walked over to the settee where she was sitting. He sat down beside her and gently, very gently, put his arm around her slender shoulders. "Why did you do it?" he asked softly. "Why did you set out to deceive me in such an elaborate way? And how could I be so blind as to not know that it was you all along?"

She turned an anxious face towards him. Her eyes had widened till they seemed to burn like green fire in her face. "I did it for revenge at first," she admitted in a small voice.

"When you wrote saying you wanted to marry one of us, and did not even bother to come down to meet us, I decided you were an arrogant beast. I still think you are in a way," she added doubtfully.

The Duke said nothing. He merely placed his

finger on her lips, and drew it gently across them. He smiled. The smile made Clorinda catch her breath. She did not know why.

"When I first married you," she continued with a visible effort at self-control, "I meant to be a good and dutiful wife. But I hadn't realized that you would just leave me alone here in the country.

"I craved the excitements of London, you see. I always envied Jack being able to stay in town. Emily and I had been brought up so quietly at Villiers Manor, that we dreamed of going into high society. We used to make up stories for one another about what we would do there—only Emily stopped when she fell in love with Robert."

"And then?" the Duke prompted.

"And then, when I was left here at the Hall, I began to think that I would go to London after all. I wanted to make you fall in love with me. So I made Emily and Robert and Jack help me.

"Well, I went to London, but I discovered that the fashionable world was not what I had thought it would be. I did not realize how heartless the flirtations could be. I hadn't realized . . . well the sort of things that could go on.

"You see," she said haltingly. "Although I talked as if I knew all about men and women, I did not really know . . . I still don't know, except that I have discovered what it feels like to love. That happened when you kissed me in Carlton House. It was so wonderful. I had not realized that a kiss could be like that."

Slowly he tightened his arm around her, and imperceptibly she turned toward him. With his other hand he gently tilted her face round toward his. He looked deeply and longingly into her eyes.

Clorinda saw his face swim before her. She could sense that he was about to kiss her again. With a little cry, she tore her eyes from his, and buried her face into the lapel of his coat.

From above her quivering body, the Duke looked gently down on her. "Come, my little dearest Clorinda," he whispered. Standing up, he drew her up with him, "You cannot ruin my coat," he teased.

She looked up at him, meeting his eyes with hers, smiling, though large tears stood on her eyelashes. His hand was tilting her face upwards. "I love you," she whispered.

With a groan he pulled her close and bent his lips to hers. At first they touched her mouth gently, then, as his passion grew, they became more insistent, more demanding.

Clorinda thought she would die in that kiss. She could feel her body melt into his. A wave of feeling took possession of her. It was as if a flame flickered into life, grew higher and stronger, till her whole being was caught up in its roaring, its searing heat . . .

With a masterful gesture, the Duke swept her off her feet. She lay, light as a feather in his strong arms, half crying, half smiling under his gaze. His breath was coming in large pants, as if he had been running for miles.

Up the long staircase, below the glittering chandeliers, the Duke carried his bride . . .

*   *   *

Later, much later, he looked down upon the slim body that was now lying beside his own—the curved small breasts, the slender flanks, the whiteness of a perfect skin. Her long lashes lay on her cheeks, hiding the glorious eyes.

As he lay there, propping himself on one elbow among the luxurious pillows in the double bed, he watched those lashes flicker—then open. The green pools of mystery that were her eyes looked wonderingly into his. A small smile hovered round her perfectly formed mouth.

"I never knew . . . it could be . . . like this," she whispered. "I did not understand that it could be so wonderful, so miraculous between men and women."

Gently he stroked back a lock of the red-gold hair that had curled over her cheek. "My darling," he said, "I did not know, myself."

"But surely?" Even in her utmost moment of bliss, Clorinda strove for the truth. "Surely, it is like this always? May I ask you?" she said anxiously. "Do not be angry."

"My love, I shall never be angry with you. You may ask what you please, my most beautiful of Duchesses. My life and my all is yours to command."

"Tell me, then," she said haltingly. "Was it like this with Lady Lancaster? If it was I feel so sorry for her now."

"It was never like this with anybody but you," said the Duke. His eyes softened as he gazed on her. With an effort he continued, "Lady Lancaster will never trouble you again. Her husband has been sent as Ambassador to Paris and she will go with him. She will enjoy Paris, I think. Are you really sorry for her?"

"I am sorry . . . for anybody . . . who loses you," came the reply.

"She never lost me, for I never belonged to her. She did not love me," said the Duke. "Oh I grant you, she was passionate enough. But passion is not the same as love. And I did not love her, my darling. Were you jealous that I might have loved another woman?"

"I am horribly jealous," confessed Clorinda.

"You should not be. Until I met the mysterious Miss de Vere I was entirely ignorant of love. You have taught me everything I know. Everything that is worth knowing. Beside it, the other women who were once in my life seem nothing."

A small hand gently nestled into his. "I? I teach *you?* The countrified Clorinda de Villiers teach the noble Duke of Westhampton about love?" Clorinda gave a small chuckle. "It is you who have taught me."

"I have taught you passion perhaps," replied the Duke seriously. "But until I met you, I had never known what love was about. I was brought up to think it was a sinful emotion. I have so much to thank you for."

A slender white arm stretched up round his neck and drew him down . . .

THE BEST OF
WARNER ROMANCES...

A WAGER FOR LOVE
by Caroline Courtney (94-051, $1.75)

The Earl of Saltaire had a reputation as a rakehell, an abductor and a ravisher of women, a dandy and a demon on horseback. Then what lady of means and of irreproachable character would consider marrying him — especially if she knew the reason for the match was primarily to win a bet? When he won a wager by marrying her, he never gambled on losing his heart.

PHILIPPA
by Katherine Talbot (84-664, $1.75)

If she had to marry for money, and Philippa knew she must, then it was fortunate that such a very respectable member of the House of Lords was courting her. It was easy to promise to "honor and obey" a man she so respected. It would be difficult, though, to forget that the man she loved and did *not* respect would be her brother-in-law . . . A delightful Regency Romance of a lady with her hand promised to one man and her heart lost to another!

LADY BLUE
by Zabrina Faire (94-056, $1.75)

A dashing Regency adventure involving a love triangle, an enfant terrible and a bizarre scheme to "haunt" a perfectly livable old castle, LADY BLUE is the story of Meriel, the beautiful governess to an impossible little boy who pours blue ink on her long blonde hair. When she punishes the boy, she is dismissed from her post. But all is not lost — the handsome young Lord Farr has another job in mind for her. Meriel's new position: Resident "ghost" in a castle owned by Farr's rival. Her new name: LADY BLUE!

THE FIVE-MINUTE MARRIAGE
by Joan Aiken (84-682, $1.75)

When Delphie Carteret's cousin Garth asks her to marry him, it is in a make-believe ceremony so that Delphie might receive a small portion of her rightful — if usurped — inheritance. But an error has been made. The marriage is binding! Oh, my! Fun and suspense abounds, and there's not a dull moment in this delightful Regency novel brimming with laughter, surprise and true Love.

SWEET BRAVADO
by Alicia Meadowes (89-936, $1.95)

Aunt Sophie's will was her last attempt to reunite the two feuding branches of the Harcourt family. Either the Viscount of Ardsmore marry Nicole, the daughter of his disgraced uncle or their aunt's inheritance would be lost to the entire family! And wed they did. But theirs was not a marriage made in heaven, but a fascinating Regency match that joined their families and fortunes while turbulent passions and pride kept them apart.

ROMANCE...ADVENTURE... DANGER...